Also by Eden Finley and Saxon Johns

Clueless Puckboy

Also by Eden Finley and Saxon James

Puckboys

Egotistical Puckboy
Irresponsible Puckboy
Shameless Puckboy
Foolish Puckboy
Clueless Puckboy
Bromantic Puckboy
Forbidden Puckboy
Possessive Puckboy
Stubborn Puckboy
Charming Puckboy

CLUELESS PUCKBOY

EDEN FINLEY & SAXON JAMES

canelo

Penguin
Random
House

First published in the United Kingdom in 2023 by Eden Finley and Saxon James

This edition published in the United Kingdom in 2026 by

Canelo, an imprint of
Canelo Digital Publishing Limited,
20 Vauxhall Bridge Road,
London SW1V 2SA
United Kingdom

A Penguin Random House Company
The authorised representative in the EEA is Dorling Kindersley Verlag GmbH.
Arnulfstr. 124, 80636 Munich, Germany

A CIP catalogue record for this book is available from the British Library.

ISBN 978 1 83598 489 5

Printed and bound in Great Britain by Clays Ltd, Elcograf S.p.A.

Look for more great books at
www.canelo.co | www.dk.com

CHAPTER ONE

QUINN

You'd think after being closeted for so many years while playing professional hockey, I'd be a lot smoother at this whole covert thing, but I'm not. Like I came out and suddenly forgot the act of subtlety. My entire demeanor is screaming up to no good, with my hoodie up, hands in my pockets, and head down as I walk from the Starbucks parking lot in Fort Erie to my destination. My secret destination.

No one can know what I'm doing. No one on the team, team management, or anyone else who works for Buffalo. Hence hopping the border into Canada.

I could talk to the guys in the Collective about it, I guess, but it's embarrassing. And Asher already gives me enough shit for it. He would never tattle on me, but I don't want to give him fresh ammunition when it comes to getting outside attention for my … groin area.

I know I'm being paranoid when I turn to make sure no one is following me, but it feels like I'm breaking the law. If anyone found out …

I cringe as I look up at the sign that hangs above the door, zeroing in on one word. *Massage.*

I feel dirty.

Shameful.

But I push my way inside anyway. Once I'm behind the safety of the darkened windows, I don't lower my hoodie. When I say no one can recognize me here, I mean it.

"Hello, Mr. Quinn," the always-smiling Chandra greets me. "He'll be right with you."

"How many times have I told you to call me Asher?"

Did I use Asher's name for my bookings? Absofuck-inglutely. I'm in Canada and paying outright; they don't need to know I'm not really Asher Quinn. Or that Asher Quinn doesn't exist, but my name is Ayri, and if you utter that name anywhere in the Buffalo Niagara area, people immediately know who you're talking about.

Go sports.

"Right. Sorry. Asher."

I tip my head to her and go sit on one of the seats where I can put my back to the door.

Overkill, maybe, but no one coming in can see my face that way.

My heart thuds as I wait for what feels like an eternity. I'm not even early. If anything, I'm late by a couple of minutes for my appointment so I can go straight in, get it done, and then get out as fast as I can.

The door to my guy's room opens, and he stands there in athleticwear. He's maybe thirty and conventionally attractive. "Ready for you." He smiles, and I follow him into the room. "Pants off. Lie down."

I strip my sweats off and lie on my back on the table.

The thing is, there's a reason I come here and put myself through all this anxiety, and it has everything to do with this guy's hands. The way he works me over. The way he's able to ease the ache between my legs.

He's worth every penny.

Joel Sutton is the best physiotherapist Canadian money can buy.

That's the lie I tell myself as he gets to work on my adductors. It has everything to do with how good he can manipulate my body and fix my aches and pains and absolutely nothing to do with avoiding having a certain team trainer's hands all over me. More important, all over my business. Near my business.

Like having a groin strain isn't embarrassing enough. Try getting a hard-on every time the professional helping goes near you.

I don't have that problem with Joel. Or any of the other team trainers. Yet, somehow, I'm always assigned to Vance Landon.

I swear, if sex had a face, it would be Vance's. If desire had a body, it would be all muscles, big hard hands, and—

Fuck, stop thinking about Vance before Joel thinks my dick is trying to hit on him.

Joel's a professional, though, and ignores my semi. Then, he presses his thumb right where the adductor muscle connects with my pelvis, and fucking fuck, holy mother of pain.

"That's tight."

As much as I like hearing that about my downstairs area, I wish it wasn't from him. Especially when I have to play tomorrow, and I need to be on top of my game.

I injured myself eight weeks ago and was assessed at a level two strain. I should be better by now, but I'm not.

And that's the other reason I'm here and not at the team facilities. Because if they find out my groin is still giving me problems, they'll bench me even more than they already have. My season has gone to shit, my pelvis aches like I'm an eighty-year-old who fell over in the snow, and I know I'm facing the very real risk of being sent back down to the AHL.

My whole life, hockey has been my dream, and I fucking made it. After I was drafted to Florida and sent to their farm team for conditioning, I was so sure it would only take me a season or two before I was called up to the big leagues. Four. It took me four years, a contract extension, and Buffalo seeing something in me and giving me a chance to get where I am, and I've only played two full seasons in the NHL. We're halfway through my third, and I don't want to get sent back down for more training.

I also don't want this to lead to a career-ending injury though.

I'm doing what I have to do to keep the life I've always wanted.

That's another lie I tell myself.

-

I dump my things in the locker room before the game and find the real Asher already warming up his legs on the bike in the workout room.

My thigh and groin feel looser today than yesterday—thank you, Joel—but I'm terrified of what condition I'll be in tomorrow.

I jump on a bike next to Asher, and he smiles over at me. Asher Dalton is … Well, he's the worst best friend I've ever had.

"I'm so happy we're playing Boston tonight and that you haven't shaved off that horrible caterpillar on your face. Ezra's going to hate it."

"It's why I keep it. It's a good-luck charm."

"By making everyone who comes face-to-face with you wonder how a child was able to grow a mustache?"

See? Worst best friend ever.

But here we are, two queer teammates, the only two queer guys on the team, so we gravitated toward each other instantly, and it's been amazing having someone close I can talk to.

Two seasons ago, I got hammered with Ezra Palaszczuk and blurted out all my relationship problems to him—mainly that the boyfriend I secretly had all through high school and while I was in the AHL dumped me because long distance was too hard once I moved to Buffalo—and so Ezra's kind of taken on this big-brother role in my life. But he's in Boston, so we don't get to see each other a lot.

Having Asher with me this season has been good for my soul. And when we're on top of our games on the ice, we're first-line material. But because of my damn pulled groin, we're suffering.

Okay, I'm suffering.

Asher's having a rookie year I can only be jealous of.

Our team has had a great season so far, so the insecurity of not contributing too is also getting to me.

I'm not only in bad physical shape but mentally as well.

"Quinn," a voice shouts across the workout room, and I freeze.

Because it's a fucking sexy voice. Everything about Vance is fucking sexy.

I hate it.

I hate him.

Okay, no, I don't hate him.

I love him.

Okay, no, I don't love him either.

I just turn into this babbling, clueless idiot around him, like I'm in junior high and I have a crush on one of the high school boys. It's embarrassing as fuck.

I turn but don't stop pedaling. "Yo."

See? Who the fuck says "yo"?

Even Asher snorts at my awkwardness.

Vance approaches me, seeing as I don't get off the bike to go to him. He's taller than me, bulkier than me, and at least five years older. He looks it, too, but in a distinguished way. Unlike me, who's twenty-four and without the ugly mustache looks sixteen.

It's why I put up with so much ribbing from every person in the NHL Queer Collective. Because I know if

I shave it off, they'll go back to calling me Baby Cheeks. Actually, I think Ezra was the only one who did that, and I only let him get away with it once. The lip sweater project started the next day.

"How's the injury?" Vance asks, but I'm too stuck in his blue eyes to answer.

So I just make random sounds instead. "Uh. Eee. Om. Oh."

Vance leans forward, glancing around me at Asher. "Are you able to translate?"

Asher laughs his head off.

I clear my throat and try again. "It's good. Making sure I'm nice and warm before going out on the ice."

"Want me to test your leg rotation? My bed's free at the moment."

Oh, fuck. It's starting already. My cock thinking about not only Vance touching me but thinking about words like *Vance's bed is ready for me.*

I force a smile while I ignore the annoying, teeny, tiny ache in my groin. "I've got it. I'm all good."

I'm getting amazing at lying to myself.

CHAPTER TWO

VANCE

I know most of the staff like to book it home as soon as the workday is done, but if there's a home game, I hang around, whether I'm scheduled for the night or not. There's something about hockey that's next-level. The smell of the ice, the speed of the players, the roar of the crowd, which is only getting bigger with every game. Buffalo is having their best season in a decade, and suddenly, everyone is a fan.

Ayri Quinn skates by, and my gaze follows him.

It always follows him.

He's … the least jocky jock to ever jock. You know, besides the swearing that he's not injured. I didn't have much to do with him until he sprained his adductor a month or so back, but the guy quickly caught my attention.

He's gorgeous, completely my type, and I'd been thanking my lucky stars that I'd never had to work on him outside of the usual bumps and bruises during a game. I knew it would take every ounce of my training to keep professional, and I was right. Only I'd underestimated just how much he'd test me.

I have never, in the history of my career, seen an athlete go so red while I was working on them. I've seen homophobes with better control. It doesn't matter how often I tell Quinn that groin injuries are ridiculously common in hockey; he just fixes his eyes on the ceiling and manages a series of noises in response to my questions.

The guy is an anomaly for a hockey player. Almost shy. Bashful. Easily embarrassed.

Though Asher fucking Dalton isn't helping when he tells everyone Quinn broke his dick.

I palm my forehead and try to get it together. It just *had* to be a groin injury.

A flash of Quinn's rigid imprint beneath his base layer passes through my mind, and I sweep it away. If I was a more confident man, I'd assume—eh, fuck it. The guy's gay as the day is long, and it's just a reaction to physical touch. Even straight guys fall victim to my magic hands, and while I haven't checked in with the other team trainers because I don't want to embarrass the guy, I can only imagine they're seeing the same side of Quinn. It's not the first badly timed boner I've had waved in my face, and it won't be the last.

Quinn gets the prize for most consistent though.

And I should get a goddamn prize for the way I'm able to block it out and just focus on my job. When he's on my table, no looking allowed. Outside of that, a little appreciation for the man is only natural.

9

He's called back to the bench, and I switch my attraction to him off as I slip back into work mode. My gaze stays pinned to him as he clears the barrier. He doesn't *look* injured, but my professional bullshitter Spidey-senses went into overdrive with him today, and I'm convinced he's lying, even if I can't prove it.

Our head trainer, Boone, says something to him, but Quinn shakes him off. When he hits the ice again, I pay closer attention. His skating is fine. His speed is lightning quick as ever. Puck handling all looks good and—what was that?

Quinn pulls to a fast stop, but his reaction time is slow. The stop, awkward, like he's favoring his right side. It's barely recognizable unless you're looking for it, but it's enough to tell me that bricks-for-brains is pushing through an injury.

Goddamn jocks never learn.

I've seen more than a handful of professional careers cut short, and it wasn't due to injury. It all came down to sheer stupidity. Quinn's adductor can be healed and strengthened, but if he won't admit there's an issue, I can't help him. And I get it. This toxic mindset that to play hockey, you need to be invincible. If you take a skate to the face or rupture a ball sac, you slap on a Band-Aid and skate harder in the next period.

It's possibly the only part of hockey I hate. Glorifying them putting their bodies on the line.

I drum my hands on my crossed arms while watching his every move, and no matter how many times Quinn puts on the brakes—whether it's gradual or sudden—I'm convinced he's being a moron.

We scrape through with the W, thanks to Dalton chipping the puck into the top corner while Boston's goalie is looking the other way, and the crowd is absolutely loving the win. The team piles on each other, and it's ridiculous how adorable I find the bear hug, but I'll be keeping that thought to myself. Can't go around emasculating the giant men with knife shoes and no teeth.

Normally I'd take off as soon as the game is over or, if it's been a busy night, jump in and help Boone out, but tonight, I've got my sights set on Quinn. That little fucker is going to admit to me that he's in pain because I can't see another player lose everything because I didn't want to step in. It's not even my personal interest in him driving me; I'd do the same for any player. He's one of the last off the ice, Dalton by his side as usual, and I fall into step beside them.

"Good game."

Dalton grunts, and Quinn doesn't say anything.

It makes my lips struggle with a smile. "How was your injury?"

"Ferfect." Quinn's eyes fly wide, and that ridiculous color splotches across his cheeks. "I mean, pine. I mean …" A frustrated sound is strangled by this throat. "Everything. Is. Okay."

Do not laugh, do not laugh.

Stay professional. He's adorable. But this is business time.

Dalton doesn't have my issues. He sniggers, and Quinn shoves him, so Dalton pushes back harder. I barely catch

Quinn before he can body-slam me into the wall. With his skates on, he's got an inch or so height on me, and the padding makes him seem enormous, but it looks like he's trying to shrink into it.

I'm used to touching his body, but not unexpectedly like this, and I let go quickly.

Quinn sends a bucketload of tension Dalton's way while Dalton strolls along, ignoring it. My hands are in my pockets as I keep pace, wondering how to make this guy spill.

"No issues with acceleration?"

He shakes his sweaty head.

"What about turns?"

"Nope."

Lying through his teeth. Wonderful. "And stops? They were smooth? Not at all painful?"

His hazel-gold eyes cut to mine. "Fine."

We reach the locker room, and I put out an arm to silently hold Quinn back while Dalton enters.

I wait until the whole team has passed, then turn to him. "Here's the thing; I don't believe you."

His stubborn mask slips, and he goes from big, bad hockey man to … nope, not adorable. Just Quinn. "What?"

"I was watching you out there. You weren't skating like you normally do."

"You, uh …" His lips twitch. "Watch? Me?"

"It's my job."

"Oh, yeah, totally, that's obviously what I mean."

How the hell does this guy get through press conferences? "Do you know where I worked before here?"

"No ..."

"College football. The star running back on our team was having issues with his ACL. He'd had two minor tears, and there was talk of pulling him for the season until he'd been through rehab. He refused. I knew he wasn't healed, but he swore black and blue that he was fine. He tore that fucker right up halfway through the season, and like that"—I snap my fingers—"career over. Goodbye, NFL. He never even got the chance to play in the big leagues. He didn't know what was truly on the line. You do."

Quinn swallows thickly, looking like a kicked puppy.

"He wasn't the first we lost to injury, but he was the first where I had a hunch he was bullshitting me." I narrow my eyes at Quinn and his guilty expression. This poor guy is a terrible liar. "Just like I have a hunch you are."

He clears his throat and shrugs, trying for an effortless smile. "I'm all good. Nothing to worry about here."

I grit my teeth. "Keep lying, dickhead. I'll get it out of you."

"Are you allowed to talk to me like that?"

"You gonna tattle on me?" I tilt my head. "Because if you did, I'd have to tell them *why* I accused you of lying."

Yeah, he doesn't like that. Just like I knew he wouldn't. But too many young, stubborn guys make the wrong choice, and I'm so fucking done watching it happen. It's their career that they're gambling with, and I get that's their issue and not mine, but it doesn't mean I'm going to sit back and do nothing.

"If I have any issues, I'll let you know," he says.

"No, you won't." I lean in. "But I'll be watching closely, Quinn. And I'm sharing my concerns with Boone."

"Wha—but. Do you have to? Like …"

Fuck me. His flustering is cute, but the goal here is to make sure he has a career to be pulled from, not stress him the fuck out.

"I'm putting together a training plan for you. Got it?"

He hurries to nod.

"And I want you back on my bed at least once a week so I can check up on tightness. Agreed?"

"Yep. Bed. Tight. Fine."

I repeat my mantra not to laugh and cuff him on the shoulder pads instead. "I can work with that."

"All right."

"Good."

"Fine."

I know I shouldn't, but I can't resist. "Ferfect."

Quinn lets out the most ridiculous squeak I've ever heard before barreling into the locker room.

Now I just have to hope he keeps up his side of the deal.

And do my best to remember my training.

CHAPTER THREE

QUINN

Like a scolded puppy, I head into the locker room to cool down, shower, and head for the treatment room so Boone can work on me.

Only, while I've been busy, Vance must've snuck in because he's in there, with Boone, and as soon as I knock, they both stop talking and stare at me like I've caught them red-handed.

He did say he was going to tattle on me to Boone, but I didn't think he meant *tonight*.

"I was hoping to get help with stretching my, uh …" My groin. "Adductor." I didn't even know that word existed until I got sick of everyone saying I pulled my groin, my dick, and everything else except for what I actually injured, which is technically a muscle in my leg. Not my penis.

I try not to look, but Vance's face is like a magnet, and the look of approval he's giving me fills my chest with fucking pride or some shit. Which is a tiny step up from the nauseating giddiness, but with his warm brown hair, dark blue eyes, and full lips constantly quirked with humor, it's impossible to keep my cool around him. Everything about the way he carries himself screams confidence, which is something I don't have a lot of.

Could I be any more pathetic? I'm thinking no.

He opens his mouth to speak, and I suck in a sharp breath because I'm sure he's about to say he can stretch it out for me, but instead, he says, "I'll leave you to it," and I deflate.

Even though having Vance's hands on me always results in me being mortified by my cock's response, the feel of his warm hands is the highlight of my week. I must be a sucker for punishment because his hands feel so good. So I'm filled with both relief and disappointment at the same time, which makes no sense.

"Hop on," Boone says. "I just want to loosen it up before we stretch it."

I climb on his table in my boxer shorts—a lesson I learned after tearing my adductor. Boxers are better than briefs. That way, I don't have to be naked in front of Vance.

Boone starts by assessing my flexibility and strength, asking me to try to push my leg out to the side while he adds resistance with his hand. "Any pain?"

"Nope."

"Are you sure?"

Boone's never asked me that before. I turn my head and eye him.

"He's worried about you," he says like it's an answer.

I mean, it is an answer, and I know exactly who he's talking about, but it annoys me. "I'm fine."

Boone's hand goes underneath my shorts, right to the joint, and presses in with his thumb. What the fuck is it with physiotherapists and trainers doing that whenever I say I'm fine?

My eyes water, but I blink back the pain. I'm not subtle enough.

"You were saying?"

"Okay, I'm still tender, but I'm doing the stretches. I'm looking after it." By cheating on you and the other team trainers with outside physiotherapy. "I promise."

"I don't need to tell you that permanent damage is on the line if you push it too far, do I?"

I swallow hard. "No."

Even though reminding me probably wouldn't hurt. It's just that between the choice of going back down to the AHL or risking it, I'd rather risk it. Tearing it for good isn't a guarantee. My career being over if I get sent backward very well could be.

Boone massages the joint and down my leg while I grit my teeth and bear it. "Let's see those stretches."

I sit up and slide off the treatment bed, and we move to the mats. I bend my good leg under me, stretch my injured leg out to my side, and rest on my elbows while moving back as far as I can.

Boone's hand lands on the small of my back, and I send up a silent thank fuck that it's Boone and not Vance. "Your back is rounding too much. Remember to keep that flat."

I want to argue that it hurts more that way, but I shut my mouth because that only proves their point. Their eyes are going to be glued to me now that Vance has pointed out I'm still not back to where I should be.

We do a couple more stretches, and I'm sent on my merry way, feeling looser than I have in a while. See, there's no issue. It just needs some TLC every now and then, and I feel amazing.

When I get to my cubby, where my after-game suit hangs, Asher's almost done dressing in the spot next to me.

"I know you losers have a tradition of meeting up whenever members of the Collective play each other, but—"

I cut him off. "You're not bailing."

"Damn it."

"What were you going to do instead? Go home and mope because your boyfriend is stuck in Vermont?"

"And if I was?"

"You have to come with me. Anton still wants to kill me after he thought something was going on with Ezra and me my rookie year, and that was, like, two years ago."

Asher laughs. "You know he only pretends to hate you because you're scared of him, right?"

"Please, save me from the wrath that is Anton Hayes."

"As long as you save me from the hands that belong to Ezra Palaszczuk."

"Deal. Besides, having you there as a buffer works. When Anton's not glaring at me, he's laughing at you for wanting nothing to do with his boyfriend anymore."

"You know, considering how many games we play per year, how is it that we seem to face Boston more than anyone else?"

I laugh. "We don't. It just feels like it."

"Let's get this shitshow over with, then."

I take out my phone to see a message from Ezra.

Hey, Quinnie, where are we meeting you and Little D for dinner?

"Where are we going to take them?" I ask Asher.

"To Niagara Falls?"

I sigh. "No, you can't push Ezra over the railing."

He grunts. "Fine. That sports bar down the road that serves Italian food. It's decorated in our colors and has signed jerseys, and considering we're kicking ass this season and just beat them, it'll be good to rub it in their faces."

I shake my head at him. "How you got your boyfriend to fall in love with you is a complete mystery."

"Hey, I agree. I think it kind of shows how fucked-up Kole really is."

Asher says that, and I get the impression he believes it. He doesn't know what Kole sees in him. Asher is big talk. Claims to have a small heart, but his heart is fucking gold. He just rarely shows it. I've seen glimpses, but to everyone, he has this tough exterior. Living in his retired NHL-playing brother's shadow might have something to do with it.

"Let's go." I text Ezra and Anton to meet us, and we're the first ones there, so we get a table at the back. The bar is full; some of the other guys from the team have come out, while most of the others went home to their families.

The guys turn up just as we get drinks for the whole table, and I get up to give Ezra a hug. Anton and Asher shake hands, but Ezra and Asher don't touch. It's a rule.

Anton gives me an up-nod with his usual glare.

Once we're all seated, everyone is quiet.

"I think this is the weirdest foursome in the entire Collective," Anton says.

"Did my boyfriend just say foursome?" Ezra looks way too excited about that.

Anton says, "You wish," at the same time Asher says, "Not fucking happening."

I can't help it. I burst out laughing. "I think Anton's right. Whose idea was it for us four to hang out?"

"Come on," Ezra says. "It's all water under the bridge. Right, Little D?"

Asher looks around, pretending he can't hear Ezra.

"Hey, at least it's entertaining for us, am I right?" I lift my beer toward Anton, who still glares. "Okay, it's entertaining for me."

Asher says Anton's joking around, but am I willing to risk a black eye to find out? No.

It's not my fault he *wrongly assumed* something happened between me and Ezra. What's even weirder is that he is fine with Asher, knowing something *did* happen between them. I'm guessing the timing has something to do with it; they weren't together then, but they were when he thought Ezra and I hooked up. It made him *feel* things, and what's worse, he showed it.

"Hey, you know how Quinn broke his dick?" Asher says. "Well, it's still not healed, and Vance, our trainer—super hot and gay, by the way—keeps making Quinn pop a boner every time he's getting a massage."

Ezra and Anton laugh while I want to bang my head on the table.

"I should've let you bail," I grumble.

"Or you could've just been nice to me."

"Don't fall for that," Ezra says. "I was nice once, and now I'm not even allowed to touch a single hair on Little D's head. Do you know how hard it is to defend the net when I'm not even allowed to block him?"

"Oh, sure, blame that on why you guys lost tonight," Asher says.

They bicker back and forth for a bit, but I tune them out. I'm too busy trying not to die of embarrassment over Anton and Ezra knowing Vance turns me on like crazy.

"Okay, I'm going to break this up before these two resort to physical violence," Anton says. "Asher, come play pool with me."

When they leave, Ezra doesn't miss a beat.

"So, your athletic trainer, huh? You going to ask him out?"

I almost choke on my beer. "Uh, how about fuck no?"

"Why not?"

"Because he's ..." Gorgeous and makes me tongue-tied, and I'm a total idiot around him. "I'm sure there are rules against it. Look at Oskar and Lane. Lane got fired from San Jose for sleeping with a player."

"True, but they also went about it the wrong way. They hid it from everyone."

My eyes widen. "Are you suggesting I ask management if I'm allowed to go out with Vance before having even so much as a proper conversation with the guy?"

"Wait, you haven't even spoken to him? What do you do when he's all up in your business?"

"Try to think of unsexy thoughts and keep my dick from getting hard. For a while, hippos wearing tutus did it. I've also gone through thoughts of my grandparents having sex, the nature channel—you know, where they're all like, 'Look at this family of cute little penguins. Now here's a huge-ass sea lion eating the babies in front of their mothers.' I'm scared I'm going to have to start thinking about snuff films and cannibalism soon. The hippos aren't cutting it anymore."

Ezra blinks at me. And then blinks some more. "Dude. You're going about this all the wrong way. Boners happen. Trainers are professionals. Just let it fly."

"Are you serious?"

Ezra touches his hand to his heart. "Oh, honey, baby Quinnie, sweetie."

"Advice without the condescension, please."

"Well, if you're not going to take my advice on fucking Vance—sorry, 'asking out' Vance—then you should 'ask out' someone else."

"And by the air quotes, I'm guessing you actually mean fuck."

"Duh. When was the last time you got laid? Maybe that's why you get so hard up around Vance. Because he's attractive, and you know he's gay."

Ezra might have a point, but I haven't had the need or desire to date again since my one and only boyfriend broke up with me. The AHL was hard enough, but moving to Buffalo was the final nail in our relationship coffin. I finally got my dream of playing in the NHL, but because of the long distance and even busier schedule—not just with more games played but with training and maintenance—it was too much for Carter. So I got the dream but lost my dream man. Or who I thought was my dream man. I've had no desire to go through that again.

It doesn't help that I'm not confident when it comes to meeting guys because I hid my sexuality for so long. It's a learned behavior to be subtle. I'm not like Ezra, who, before Anton, would go up to guys and just say, "Wanna fuck?" and then go do it.

I'd probably say, "Fanna Wuck?"

I want to sink into my seat and drown in my beer. "Maybe I'll try asking someone else out."

"And when you say ask someone out …" Ezra encourages.

"I mean have sex."

"Good boy." He reaches over and pats my head.

I didn't really just agree to that, did I?

CHAPTER FOUR

VANCE

I whistle along to the sound of Radioactive blasting in my ears as I check the stock in the treatment room. We're good for the day, and it won't be long before players start showing up for training. Boone won't be in until later, but I should have O'Hennessy as backup before the masses converge with face wounds, tender ribs, and sprains and strains from last night's game.

A loud yawn rips from me as I turn toward the doorway and find Quinn hovering in it.

I pull out one of my earbuds. "You're in early."

He shrugs awkwardly. "Do you … uh …"

I grin and wave toward the table. "Climb on up."

"You sound like a doctor."

"Cool. I've always wanted to be called Dr. Landen."

Quinn goes to say something else but bites it off. He's stiff as he moves to the table, partially strips off, and climbs up onto it. And the stiffness isn't being caused by his injury.

I mentally switch over to professional mode.

"You hate being worked on, don't you?"

"Something like that," he mutters.

I start with some gentle leg stretches as I work my way up his thigh. His muscles feel strong, and everything's going smoothly until I reach midthigh. That's when it always happens; Quinn grows hard, and I turn my focus to nothing but his thigh. I'm not lying when I say erections are natural, that they happen a lot, but I've been trained to ignore them. It just happens to take *all* my training to ignore something that almost pokes my eye out every single time he's on my table. Quinn is hands down the biggest challenge of my career.

But I'm a professional, and I'm able to keep focus on the muscle that needs it until—

"... Miss Piggy jerking off Kermit the Frog ..."

My gaze shoots up to Quinn's face. His eyes are screwed shut, and his lips are moving, but I can't make out anything else.

Did ... did he ...

Okay, this is getting ridiculous. I let go of him to grab a chair and drag it to the side of the bed, and then I sit down, elbows propped on my knees, and wait. It takes him a minute more of rambling about "toe cheese"—something I *never* want to think about—and "beetle *something*"—that I straight up don't wanna know—before he squints open one eye.

"Hi."

He clears his throat and hurries to sit up. "Yeah, hey. We done?"

"Nope."

25

"Then …" Those vivid eyes skirt the room, but I patiently wait for them to land on me again. "What, uh … what are you doing?"

"You're uncomfortable."

"*No.*" The unconvincing way he says that makes me laugh.

"I'm here to help you. I don't want you to dread every time you have to come see me."

"I don't … it's not that."

"Then what is it?"

He shakes his head, goldish-blond hair flopping with the movement.

"Well, if you won't tell me, that's the only conclusion I've got." I have no clue if Quinn just goes around popping boners for all the team trainers, and I'm not about to ask, but if his issue is inconvenient bodily reactions, he needs to get over it. He's in pro sports. He showers naked in front of his teammates. Dresses in front of them. Sure, neither of those things requires him to be touched, but after the great win last night, I'd be shocked if he didn't go out and get a release to celebrate. That's what most of the single players do. Unless … he isn't single. I haven't given it much thought before, but if he isn't, that makes my attraction even more uncomfortable. Actually, I know next to nothing about him outside of this job, and maybe that's why he's struggling.

"I'm thirty," I say when it's clear he isn't going to talk. "Played a bit of sports in high school but wasn't good enough to get scouted for college. Love being fit and active though, and when I ran through what I wanted to do with the rest of my life, I knew it was going to be something in the sports industry. This wasn't an easy job to get, but I knew a friend of a friend in management, and they hooked me up with an interview." I pause when Quinn peeks up at me from under his eyelashes and offer him a friendly smile. "I like music and going to concerts, love watching the team play, catching up with my friends, and going to the gym. I came out in college, which went pretty smoothly ..."

His eyebrows twitch in a frown at that.

I lower my voice. "Your coming out wasn't so smooth?"

Quinn huffs. "Not ... not totally. I only officially came out a year ago. Two years to a few of the Collective guys, and my parents and sister knew in high school. They were all fine, but I was terrified of what my team would think. Apparently, my long-term boyfriend couldn't handle the distance and was over the secrecy because he dumped me right as I hit the NHL level."

"Damn, I'm sorry."

"Yeah, well, it wasn't fair on him."

I consider that. "It's a bit more complicated though, isn't it?"

"What do you mean?"

"Well, did he know you had no plans to come out? Did you somehow lead him to believe it would be different?"

Quinn hesitates. "No. He knew that while I was in the AHL, I couldn't do anything. Hockey was my dream. It's more inclusive now, but things aren't perfect. If it was a choice between two good players, one straight one and one gay one, guess who's going to have the least impact on team dynamics?"

It hurts that it's something Quinn even had to consider at all. Though it's just occurring to me that this is the most amount of words he's ever spoken to me without fumbling all over himself, and I want that to continue.

"From where I'm sitting, you were both asking something of the other person that they didn't want to give. You wanted him to stay in the closet, and he wanted you to come out and move closer. Both of those things are a personal decision. No one was at fault. Just wasn't your time, maybe."

He rubs his fingers over his opposite knuckles. "Yeah. Sometimes it's a relief though."

"That's good, I guess."

"Means if I do get thrown back into the AHL, the only person I'm letting down is me." Quinn manages an awkward laugh that doesn't hit.

"You're an amazing player. You really think they'd do that?"

"Well ..." He gestures toward his groin. "Who knows?"

The pieces click into place. He's not trying to play through the pain to prove something to people; he's doing it so he doesn't lose his place on the team. From everything I've heard, management is happy with him, but then, not a lot gets filtered down to us.

I shift forward in my chair and give his knee a supportive squeeze, pulling back right away instead of leaning into my urge to linger. "I get it."

"Y-you do?" His eyes are wide as saucers.

"It's simple. You don't want this injury to get eyes on you. Or having people questioning whether you should still be here."

"Right."

"So let me help you."

Quinn groans. "I set myself up for that."

"Sure did." I stand and slap his good thigh. "Now, up you get. I told you I was going to work on some rehab exercises for you, and I stayed up last night doing exactly that."

"You did?"

"I don't know whether the shock in your voice is because you think I'm shit at my job or you don't think you're worth the effort. Either way, you're wrong on both counts. Come on."

Once he's got his shorts back on—thank God—I lead Quinn out to the training rooms and set up a place in the corner. There's still another half an hour before the team is supposed to be in here, so I'm not sure why Quinn turned up so early, but I'm not going to send him away until then in case he changes his mind. Which is a very real possibility.

I'm also selfishly not hating this one-on-one time.

I grab a ball and point to the mat. "Lie down."

He does as directed, and then I get him to bend his knees and put the ball between them.

"I want ten glute bridges, thirty seconds each time. But you need to squeeze the ball using your adductors while you do it."

"Okay."

"And tell me if it goddamn hurts."

Fuck me, that almost gets a smile out of him. We walk through each of the exercises I've drawn up, and the more focused he gets, the more Quinn forgets to be tense and awkward. I let myself enjoy the rare glimpse of him humaning.

We make it all the way to the last exercise without any blushing or stammering or *Kermit the Frog* moments.

"You're doing good. Last one. How's it feeling?"

I can tell he's about to say "fine" when he changes his mind. "Tight. But not sore."

"Perfect. On your side this time. You're going to run through some side planks with assistance. This will be the hardest one you do today, but if we can do it a few times a week, we'll get that muscle all loosened up in no time."

"M–my muscle?"

Has he somehow missed the whole point of this? "Your left adductor."

"Yeah. Right. Obviously."

His face is looking red by the time he lies on his side. I didn't think I'd worked him that hard today, but maybe he's putting more strain on it than I thought. "Sure you're ready?"

"Yes," he grunts.

"Okay, I want all your weight on one hand and your lower foot, then I'm going to gently lift your top leg.

Once I have you supported, you need to control lowering your hip to the ground and back up again. Got it?"

"Yep."

I stand behind him and wrap a hand under his lower leg and one just above his knee. "Ready."

Quinn pushes up onto his hand, and I lift his leg at the same time. There's slight resistance, but once he's settled, he lowers his hip to the ground slower, then presses it back up again. These side planks are great for his core muscles as well as his adductors, and getting all those muscles working together at the same time is the key to his recovery. Without that, he'll continue to favor one side until he fucks that up too.

I glance down to check his form and—oh no. The poor guy just can't catch a break. He must be so hard up for sex that this simple touch sets him off.

He's confirmed he doesn't have a boyfriend, but I get the sense he's not like the other single guys on the team either. I find myself inappropriately wondering how long it's been since he's let himself indulge.

Jesus, how long has it been since *I* indulged?

His whole body has gone stiff again, his movements thrown off. I really need to do something about his embarrassment.

I just need to say something to set him at ease. *Looks like you're enjoying this* probably isn't the one though. *My dick gets hard sometimes too* also straddles that creepy line.

Except while I'm busy stewing over what the hell to say to make him comfortable, I leave it too long.

Asher Dalton walks in, gear bag slung over his chest, takes one look at the pair of us, and hesitates for the briefest second before sniggering and moving on.

Quinn jerks in my hold, falling forward, and my hand slips …

And slips …

My knuckles graze his shaft, and a sharp spear of heat passes through me.

I step back, hands raised and trying not to get hard, as Quinn topples to the ground.

"Shit, I'm so … I'm *so* sorry." I move to crouch beside him, but there's no way in hell I can touch him right now. "Are you okay?"

"Fline. *Fine*." He scrambles away from me, face blazing red. "I'm gonna …"

I stand there watching him run after Dalton, heart sinking as I realize all the progress we made this morning is probably down the drain.

CHAPTER FIVE

QUINN

"You're a disaster," Asher says as soon as I get to our side-by-side cubbies.

"No thanks to you."

"Sorry, but seeing your huge dick imprint threw me for a second. I didn't know if I walked in on porn or a treatment."

My face burns. "Ugh. You're right. I am a disaster. You need to take me out tonight after practice."

"I really, really like you as a friend, but you know I—"

"Not on a date, you asshole. Be my wingman. I need to hook up."

Asher watches me for a beat. "I didn't realize you did that. Random hookups."

I don't. "Ezra told me I should get over my crush on certain athletic trainers by getting under other hot men."

Asher's silent, and as I glance at him to see why, his eyes are wide, glancing just above my head.

I slump and whisper, "Vance is behind me, isn't he?"

Asher's green eyes meet mine. "He was."

"Did he hear me?"

33

"I'm sure he didn't."

"Why don't I believe you?"

"We should definitely go out tonight. I never thought I'd see the day I'd agree with Ezra, but you need to get over Vance."

"Okay, Vance totally heard me, freaked out, and ran away."

Asher's features soften for one of his rare moments of letting his heart show. "Forget about him. We'll go out tonight, and you can meet someone new."

Someone new. Finding myself a man. Putting myself out there.

Why do I want to throw up?

More importantly, why am I terrified to turn around and see Vance still listening even though Asher says he's not.

With a deep breath, I turn to my cubby and fight the urge to climb inside it and hide. I don't though. I keep turning to find no one behind me.

Vance isn't there. He's not there during practice either. Or afterward when we go to Boone to get strapped, massaged, and whatever else we need done to us.

I should be relieved, but instead, I'm questioning if he disappeared because of what I said. Or maybe he didn't hear it at all. Yeah, let's keep thinking that. I have to. Otherwise, my headstone will read "died of embarrassment."

When we're showered and dressed, Asher slaps my shoulder. "Ready?"

"As ready as I'll ever be."

He grins. "So not at all?"

"Pretty much."

"Tonight is going to be fun." And supportive Asher is gone again.

"Where are we going?" I ask.

"I'd normally suggest going to this drag bar Kole and I like to go to when he's in town, but that's more low-key than I think you need. There's a seedy-looking underground gay club that is perfectly trashy. Let's go there."

"Perfect."

"You don't mean ferfect?"

"I fucking hate you," I grumble.

He throws his arm around my shoulders. "I love you too."

"I didn't even know you were capable of saying the L word. I'm impressed."

"I only say it to those I take pity on."

"Soooo, your boyfriend?"

"Yep. I pity him for having to put up with me."

"So do I."

"Let's get out of here."

—

Twenty minutes later, Asher parks his car in a shitty part of town.

"How did you find this place?"

"Have you heard of this thing called Google? It's great for looking up things."

"Okay, I'll rephrase. Why were you googling seedy underground bars? Should I worry about you and Kole?"

He snorts. "I was looking up a place I could take him when he visited. If it were up to me, we wouldn't leave the bedroom whenever I get the chance to see him, but I need him to fall in love with this city so he moves here when he's done with med school. Hence why I took him to the fun drag bar instead of this place."

"That's … actually one of the most romantic things I've ever heard." I reach over and ruffle his hair. "You do have a heart. A big, full—"

"You tell anyone, I'll kill you in your sleep."

For the first time in a while, I'm able to laugh at him and not the other way around. But as soon as we enter the bar, I get the impression that'll change again fast.

Because I'm so out of my depth.

And yep, there's Asher's laugh. He leans in to yell over the doof doof music filling my veins. "Let's get you a drink first. Or six."

Yes, please.

Asher orders us shots of all things, and I'm glad we have a light weights day tomorrow before our next road trip.

I down the shots he feeds me, waiting for the buzz to take over, but it's possible my nerves are consuming all the alcohol because nothing happens.

"Selfie time," Asher says.

Asher is so not the selfie type, and I'd put money down that in any unofficial photo, he's giving the finger to the camera, so when he lifts his phone and takes a smiling photo of us, I give him a perplexed look.

"Messaging Kole where I am so he knows why I haven't called him yet."

"He's got you on a tight leash."

Asher sends a glare my way. "Tell anyone I said this—"

I roll my hand. "And you'll kill me. Got it. Go on."

"Kole doesn't ask me to do it, but long distance is hard, so I'm open about everything I'm doing and when. It's called *communication*."

Maybe that's what my issue with Carter was. Instead of keeping those communication lines open, we did our own thing and gave each other our time whenever we weren't busy. Which, as an AHL hockey player dating a college student, was basically never.

He's the only relationship I've known, and we started when we were teenagers.

It's no wonder I'm flailing in the sex and love department. The only guy I've been interested in since Carter is off-limits.

Asher nudges me. "Don't bust a blood vessel, dude. You look like you're thinking way too hard."

My lips quirk. "I'm just terrified to be living in a world where Asher fucking Dalton is in a healthy, respectful relationship and I'm not."

Asher throws his head back and laughs. "You and me both."

We finish our drinks and turn around, facing the dance floor while leaning back on the bar.

It's definitely a hookup kind of bar, not too busy, but it's loud and dark.

A guy across the room catches my eye. He looks put together, maybe a little older than me, but not by much. He's clean-shaven, attractive, and when we lock eyes, it's as if he's trying to have a silent conversation with me.

He tips his head, and I return it on reflex. Then I almost have a heart attack as he makes his way over to us.

When he reaches me, Asher turns his back on us, pretending he's not paying attention when I know for certain that he is.

"Hey," the guy says.

"Hi."

"Nice stache."

See, I knew it made me look older. Maybe not more sophisticated, but definitely older. "Thanks."

"I'm a sub."

"Oh, nice! I bet it's hard, but playing with the kids is probably fun."

He frowns. "What?"

I lean in and repeat myself, louder this time. His expression only becomes more horrified though.

Beside me, Asher's body quivers with laughter, and that's when I know I've fucked up.

So *not* a substitute teacher, then?

The guy, either too confused or wondering if he should call the police, stands there with his mouth opening and closing like a fish.

Asher turns around and leans across me. "He's a good guy. Just too innocent for his own good."

This time, my smile is forced and shows way too many teeth.

"Sorry. Innocent isn't my thing." My potential hookup stalks away, and my heart deflates.

Asher's hand touches my shoulder. "Definitely not the guy for you to do this with."

Another guy approaches, and I stand straighter, trying to put on a mask of enthusiasm like I did when I was a teenager and applied for a job at the local Dairy Queen. Only, this guy goes straight past me and right to Asher.

"Hi. Do you want—"

Asher puts his hand on the guy's chest to gently push him out of his personal space and yells, "Eat shit and die."

He needs to stop telling people that. Management has already talked to him about being rude to the fans.

The guy puts up his hands and stalks away.

"This is hopeless," I say.

"Let's try the dance floor. Come on, I want to see you bust a move."

If sidestepping could be considered busting a move, I'm a pro.

Asher and I dance together, messing around, and it's the first time all night I'm actually able to relax. Asher's dropping some of his tough exterior too. At least when it comes to me. I like this side of Asher, and it's moments like this where I'm reminded of why he's my best friend on the team. He doesn't have to be here. He's here for me.

Guys try to dance with him, but he's like a ninja when it comes to outmaneuvering them and somehow shoving me in their direction. They're not interested in me though. I try not to take it to heart, especially when

Asher's as gorgeous as he is. Bright green eyes and the permanent kind of scowl that makes you want to fix whatever's broken inside him.

And then, when I least expect it, a large hand wraps around my waist, and a bigger body presses against my back.

I freeze for a second but then lean into it, sending Asher a silent question about the guy's face. Not that looks are important with this kind of thing. Asher throws me a thumbs-up and dances away, casually leaving me to my random guy.

Our hips move together, he grinds against my ass, and … I'm actually getting into it. Really into it.

He leads, and I like that. I don't have to think. I can feel how hard he is against me, and my own dick responds in kind. We grind, sinking lower and lower, and even though there's a twinge, a pinch, in my adductor, I go with him because I'm living for the friction between us.

But as I try to push back against him and bend my knees for more, something in my groin pulls. I swear I feel a pop. My leg goes out from underneath me, and flashbacks to the night I strained my adductor come flooding back.

Next minute, I'm on the dirty, sticky floor, in pain, terrified I just fucked my entire career.

I can't breathe, the pain is that bad, and I grit my teeth.

How in the fuck can I play hockey on this injury and be fine, but try to grind up against a guy, and the whole thing tears?

Or, it at least feels like it has.

Motherfucker, this hurts more than when I first strained it on the ice.

Asher's face appears over me. "Fuck, dude, what happened?"

"My leg. My adductor again."

Then, the last person I'm expecting or wanting to see steps up beside Asher, and I think I'm hallucinating. Warm brown hair haloing his head, light brown eyebrows quirked in concern.

"V–Vance?" I stutter.

He shakes his head at me. "You're an idiot."

CHAPTER SIX

VANCE

I'd promised myself that following Quinn and Dalton to this seedy bar was purely for the sake of curiosity. To keep an eye on them. It's not stalking if I don't get caught.

Which sounds like exactly the type of reasoning a stalker would use.

And yet here I am, locked eyes with a player who's under my immediate care and apparently has a fucking crush on me.

Which makes it really, *really* hard to ignore this attraction I have to him.

But the last thing I'm going to do is embarrass the poor guy by telling him I overheard. Especially when we can never happen. If the team and NHL weren't a thing and I met Quinn randomly in a bar, I'd definitely take him home. He's hot as hell, and the adorable stuttering and awkwardness he has around me suddenly makes sense. I shake free my thoughts. Either way, I'm not going to acknowledge his crush when it opens too many ethical problems.

And yet, when I overheard, I promptly followed him here. *Definitely no ethical problems there, genius.*

"What are you doing here?" Dalton asks suspiciously.

I ignore him, crouching down beside Quinn. The random guy he was dancing with has disappeared, clearly not wanting to deal with this mess. "How bad's the pain?"

"About an eight," he says through gritted teeth. "But my embarrassment's at a twelve."

"I'd be surprised if it was any less." I offer up a friendly smile. "Think you can get out to the car?"

"I've been drinking."

I huff a laugh. "Yeah, it's the alcohol I'm concerned about and not your adductor." Fucking hockey players.

"Asher drove anyway."

Dalton lifts his hands like he's innocent. "Also been drinking. I'd planned to order a car to pick us up."

"Then I guess it's lucky I have mine and I *haven't* been drinking."

I hook my arm around Quinn, taking in the scent of sweat and locker room soap, and nod at Dalton to get on his other side. Quinn might be smaller than me, but he's still big and heavy, and there's no way I could carry him out of here without causing him a world of pain.

Supported by us both, Quinn hops on his good leg toward the exit. He'll still be putting strain on the muscle, but there's not a lot we can do in this situation.

When we reach the car, I send Dalton back into the bar to grab some ice in a towel or something else he can bring out here, then help Quinn onto the back seat. I lay him down, leg propped up on the center console, then get him to undo his jeans and drag them down under his ass. And thank fuck he's not hard for once. Pain for the win.

"You good?"

"Mortified." He grunts. His eyes are screwed closed against the pain, hand resting over his thigh, like he's fighting with himself over grabbing the injury and leaving it the hell alone.

"That was, uh … some dance moves." I could imagine myself in that random dude's position, and I wanted so badly to cut in. Maybe if I had, it wouldn't have ended how it did. "I was a fan until you dropped to the floor."

He doesn't reply, just makes a kind of throaty sound.

"I bet I'm probably the last person you wanted to see—"

"You have no idea," he mutters. And hey, if I hadn't heard him earlier, I might be offended, but I'm finally starting to understand the avoidance. The bashfulness. *Fline.*

I've never had a guy get flustered over me before, but I really, really like it. Especially from him. Maybe too much from him.

"But I'm on your side, remember? Same team." I laugh and point toward the bar, where Dalton is pushing through the door. "Technically, we're on two of the same teams. And between you and me, we need more queer players in the sport." I drop my voice so Dalton doesn't hear. "You're not leaving the team so easily, Ayri."

His eyes snap open and meet mine. Having him look at me so directly sends something skittering across my chest.

"I've got you," I try to assure him.

"Ice." Dalton thrusts a glass in front of my face.

"How'd you get this outside?"

"I took the glass, and I walked out with it."

"No one stopped you?"

"The good thing about having resting I'll-cut-you face is that people tend to leave you alone."

I pass the glass to Quinn, ignoring Dalton's ... *Dalton-ness*. "Hold this on the site of the pain. I'm going to take you home and check you over, okay?"

"O-okay."

My gaze cuts to Dalton. "You coming?"

"Better not." He shakes his phone my way. "The old ball and chain needs me to report in. He's a real hard-ass. Totally controlling. Hates when I'm out too long."

"Right ..."

"You two have fun now." He backs away, and for the first time around me, he cracks a smile. And if I thought the smile would soften his features, I'm wrong because it only makes him look downright evil. "Look after my boy, Vance."

And fuck. He definitely knows I overheard them earlier. I thought I'd played it off well.

I'm tempted to flip him the bird, but even though I'm not at work, I still have to be professional. It's ridiculous how much I have to remind myself of that.

I jump in the front of my RAV4 and have Quinn direct me to his place. It's not far from KeyBank Center, and he has me pull up in the driveway of a two-story house with a wide front porch.

"This is nice," I say as I open the back door and help him climb out. He's moving stiffly and gritting his teeth against the pain.

"Yeah, well, it's got nothing on Ezra and Anton's place, but …"

"But what?" I hook an arm around him and kick the door closed behind me. He puts way too much weight on me as we walk, which makes me think this could be worse than I assumed.

"I didn't want to jinx anything," he says at last.

It hurts that he has so little confidence in himself when he's a goddamn NHL player. And he's fucking good too. That's not just my bias showing. When Quinn's having a good night, he cleans up on the ice. If he could get out of his own way, he'd be a star player.

"As much as I want to continue this conversation, I get the feeling making it down the icy path and up those few stairs without you slipping is going to take all my energy."

He gives me a strained laugh. "Fuck my life."

"If you weren't so heavy, I could carry you." I'm bigger but only marginally, and he's all muscle.

"You … you …" He blinks at me, cheeks reddening, and I can't believe I didn't see it before. He's not exactly subtle about his crush. This is going to make it so much harder to keep my thoughts to myself. When things were one-sided, it was easy to push the thoughts away, but knowing he'd be down for some fun is way too tempting.

Quinn tries to keep his leg as immobilized as possible, half his weight on me and the other half on his good leg.

The house isn't what I'd have expected for an NHL player, but then my only real knowledge is when one of the guys on the teams buys a place and wants to show off pictures. Mostly huge family homes and a few sleek apartments.

Quinn's place is older-style, with fancy wood floors and white paneling.

I help lower him onto the couch, then prop his leg up on the arm, stuffing every cushion I can find under it.

"How's that?"

"Fine."

"Not fline?"

"Hey, fuck you."

I laugh and use the last cushion to gently hit him over the head. "Lean forward."

"Not sure I want to after that abuse."

"Considering not listening to me led you here, you should probably do as you're told from now on."

He huffs but leans forward so I can stuff the pillow behind his head.

I move to the kitchen and rummage around for a towel, some ice packs, and some anti-inflammatories. When I walk back into the room and set it all down, even without looking, I can feel Quinn's eyes on me. And when I glance over my shoulder, sure enough, his golden stare is … well, it's on my ass, but only for a second before it sweeps up my body and comes to rest on my face.

"Umm, do you ..." he starts. "Should I take off my jeans?" The sweet creases on his forehead make me smile.

"It'd probably be easier for the cold pack, but up to you."

"You don't need to ... you know, check it?"

"Not tonight. It's hurt—we don't need to know much more at this point. Your only focus tonight is to stop moving it as much as possible. You're going to ice it for twenty, then I'll wrap it before I go."

"Wrap it?"

It's hard not to laugh at the way he swallows. "This isn't your first time at this," I point out.

"Yeah, I know." He scowls. "Boone is going to kill me. And Coach. And management."

"So dramatic." I hand over the ibuprofen. "Take these."

He does it without complaint, and then I drop down into the armchair across from him as he struggles out of his jeans.

"Need help?"

"I got it."

Still so fucking stubborn, but it's probably for the best.

He gets them completely off one leg but can't push them all the way off the other. His movement has me concerned this is more than just a strain. If he's torn his adductor, he's in for a heavy recovery. I'm not about to mention that now though. He'll lose his shit.

I wait him out, and eventually, Quinn stops struggling and falls back into the cushions. "I've changed my mind."

"Shocking."

"Ever been told that you can be condescending?"

I smirk as I cross back over to him. "Surprisingly, only by you."

His eyes are locked on the ceiling as I gently lift his heel, slide his jeans off, then set his leg back carefully again. The blond hairs brush my fingertips, and if there's one thing Quinn has going for him, it's that he has incredible calves.

I leave him to ice his groin and duck out to the car to grab an elastic bandage from my kit. It'll do a lot to keep his adductor supported if he chooses to ignore my warnings about keeping his damn ass on the couch.

And sure enough, as soon as I walk back inside, he's stretched out halfway across to his coffee table, reaching for the remote.

I grab both his shoulders to force him back and retrieve the remote myself, but just as I'm about to hand it over, I jerk it back from his grip.

"Am I going to be able to trust you here by yourself?"

"What do you mean?"

I wave the remote at him. "I'm serious. No movement."

"What if I need to piss?"

"Then do it in your goddamn pants for all I care."

He scowls. "You're the worst nursemaid ever."

"Lucky that wasn't my career choice, then."

He won't look at me, and that's fair enough because I'm not exactly being all kind and caring. But I tried that route, and look at where it got him.

"Do you have someone who can stay and help you?"

"No."

I bite off my annoyance. "I can get you the number of a home nurse, but it won't be until tomorrow."

"I don't need a nurse."

"You're being a baby."

"Are you serious?" He shoves up to sitting, and I push him right back down again.

He's red in the face, but it's not from blushing this time. "All I wanted was to go out and hook up for a fucking change, and I can't even do that. I'm stuck here until my injury heals, and who the hell knows when that will be, and the only person I have in this stupid city is Asher, and asking him to come and wait on me hand and foot is the equivalent of asking a grizzly bear to pet it."

I can't help it—I laugh. "I'm sorry, but that's a visual."

"Glad you're amused." He actually crosses his arms.

I sigh and pull the table closer so I can sit on the edge. "Haven't you been listening? He's not the only person." Even though it goes against all my better judgment, I say, "I'll stay tonight. Make sure you're fed and help you to the bathroom and whatever you need. I'll talk to Boone in the morning about taking you down there or whether it's better to send a doctor up here. Then we can decide whether you need a nurse or not."

"How bad do you think this is?"

"What was your pain number the first time you hurt it?"

"A ... four?"

"Right." I try to convey with my stare that this is unlikely to be a strain, and I hate the way the light in his eyes dims.

"*Fuck.* Can we at least agree not to tell the team I did it *dancing*? Can we say I went for a run or, fuck, I was having sex? Sex injury would get me sympathy and man points, right?"

"That's all good and well, but one, would Asher keep that a secret? And two, why would I have been there if you were having sex?" I realize I've said the wrong thing right after I say it because his cheeks flame red, and all it does is project images of the two of us onto me. I clear my throat. "No point stressing about it now. Let's take it a step at a time." I reach down and remove his ice pack. "I'm going to strap it, then we'll ice it again in three to four hours."

He nods but doesn't answer me.

I press the wrap to his inner thigh, and Quinn immediately hisses. Yeah, not good. I take my time, gently winding the elastic bandage around his beefy thigh, up over his hip, under his back, ignoring the glimpse of abs as I cross his front, and bring it back around his thigh again.

His skin is warm. Soft. His upper thighs are smooth and hairless and so damn— *Professional! I need to be professional.*

It's next to impossible, though, because of this simmering energy between us. There's always been a vibe, an attraction to him, but I thought his babbling was because he was uncomfortable with touch or with me as a person. Knowing it's because he's attracted to me too …

I swear he doesn't breathe the entire time I wrap his injury.

I'm not so sure I do either.

CHAPTER SEVEN

QUINN

Note to self: Vance has a stubborn streak. No matter how many times I tell him to take my bed upstairs, he refuses and sleeps on a makeshift bed made up of blankets and pillows on my living room floor.

Because that's not going to make me obsess all night and not get any sleep at all.

It's totally what happens.

And every time I move slightly, he wakes up. World's lightest sleeper ever. He jumps up and is all, "What can I get you?"

"Nothing. I'm just damn uncomfortable." This is why I should've gotten a place with a downstairs bedroom.

I do need to take a leak, but asking him to help me go to the bathroom is even more mortifying than spraining my groin again—possibly even tearing my adductor— while dancing with some random guy.

Fuck my life.

I wish I could wait until Vance leaves, but I know I can't because he's made it clear if he's not babysitting me, someone else will be. Though I do wish it was Asher who was here to see me take a piss instead of Vance.

Then again, on no planet would Vance ever be attracted to a bumbling idiot like myself, so really, there's nothing to ruin the romance between us because it doesn't exist.

"I need to use the bathroom," I relent.

"You have two options. I can grab an empty bottle or milk carton, or I can help you to the bathroom and hold you up while you piss."

"Is there an option three where I get to keep just a shred of dignity?"

He pretends to think about it. "Do you honestly have any left after breaking your dick on the dance floor?"

I glare at him. "You sound like Asher."

"I'm a health professional, Quinn. I'm here to help."

"And just when I thought you'd seen me at my worst." I close my eyes. "Fine. Empty what's left in my gallon of milk in the fridge. I think it's out of date anyway."

He gets up and goes to my kitchen, opens the fridge, but then also opens drawers. "You got scissors?"

"What for?"

"I've been near your dick enough to know the tiny hole at the top isn't gonna cut it."

Jesus H. Christ. Kill me now.

"So much for being professional," I call out.

"Just stating facts. Ah, found some." There's more rummaging around, and then he comes back with the top of the container cut off. "Here you go."

I grumble as I take the container to do my business. "Could you turn around at least?"

He laughs and turns his back to me and then whistles while the sound of peeing into the container fucking echoes around the place.

"I'm done."

He turns. "I'll take it."

I hand it over and die inside.

Vance takes it to the bathroom to flush it. The sound of water running joins the roar of the toilet, and then he brings the carton back empty and places it on the floor by my side. "In case you need it again."

"Thank you," I mumble and avoid eye contact with him.

He sits on the coffee table again, leaning toward me like he's going to force me to look at him. It works. The moment I meet his dark blue eyes, shivers rattle my gut.

"What can I do to make you more comfortable around me?" he asks, like it's that fucking simple.

Ezra seems to take over my mind as my first thought is to say *suck my dick*. Thankfully, I have more self-restraint than Ezra does.

"I wish I knew," I say. "When I'm around y—" I can't say him because then I may as well be confessing my stupid feelings that are stupid and juvenile. "Authority figures, I'm nervous."

Vance smiles. "I'm not an authority figure."

"You're not exactly my equal."

"I could argue you actually outrank me. They can fire me and have a replacement in a second if you asked them to."

"You could bench me indefinitely if you wanted to."

"Hmm, technically, that would be Boone and the team doc."

"On your advice."

"If I'm advising it, it would be for a legitimate reason."

I lower my voice. "I know."

"Would talking about myself help you relax more? That worked the other day, didn't it?"

It did. A little. But it also made me like him even more because I was getting something real. Even if it was superficial background stuff, it made him more dimensional than just the hot trainer who has to put his hands on me.

"I guess."

"What if I even the playing field?" The look on his face scares me.

And then? My inner Ezra bursts out of me before I can rein it in. "You're not going to drop trou and tell me to rub your groin, are you?" My eyes widen, and my mouth drops, shocked I allowed that out. "Sorry. That sounded way dirtier out loud than it did in my head, and I didn't mean—"

Vance bursts into laughter. "See, like that. Saying that stuff isn't going to get you into trouble with me, so you can say it, and I'll still be professional."

I eye him because part of me was still sure he'd heard I had a crush on him, but now I'm pretty certain he didn't.

Otherwise, he wouldn't be encouraging my awkward form of flirting, and that's a slippery slope.

Okay. So he didn't hear me.

He doesn't know I have a crush on him.

And he sees me as something so completely out of the realm of sexual that me asking to take his pants off and massage him doesn't even register on the sexy scale.

Well, don't I feel like I'm drop-dead fucking gorgeous?

I'm saved from saying something equally unsexy to Vance when my doorbell rings. "It's early. Who's that?"

Vance jumps up. "I'll get it."

When he walks to the door, I'm both relieved and annoyed when Asher says, "Oh. Helloooo," in a very drawn-out way.

"Good. You're here," Vance says. "I'm going to make some calls while you sit in there with him and make sure he doesn't move."

"Really? Babysitting duty? I just came by to see if he was okay."

"He's not, and he's refusing to stay still."

"Is tying him up a possibility? I'm great with knots."

"Fuck off, *Little D*," I call out, knowing he hates that nickname.

"And just for that, you're on your own," he yells back.

"Go. Living room. Now," Vance says with a sexy growl to his voice. Damn him.

Asher enters and waggles his eyebrows at me. I roll my eyes back because yes, obviously my dream man and I hooked up last night when I'm in so much pain I can't move.

Asher Dalton is a pastel crayon. Pretty, but not very bright.

"Are you any better this morning?" he asks, letting his genuine side show.

"I'm in less pain than last night, but it still hurts."

"More than the first time?"

"I think I'm fucked."

He goes to open his mouth when I put my hand up to stop him.

"And no. Not by Vance, smartass."

"What's the plan?"

"I dunno. I'm assuming another scan to check to see if I tore it. If I did …" Fuck, if it's a tear, it could be the end for me in the NHL. They'll skip over sending me back down to the AHL. I'd be done.

"We're not going to think about that," Vance says, entering the room again, phone still in his hand. "Boone is calling Doc Travers. Thinks we'll have to get you checked out to make sure there isn't a tear."

I glance at Asher. "See?"

"Which means, up you get and in the car," Vance says. "Dalton, so glad you volunteered to help."

Asher stands. "I'd love to, but I have this rule about people who hear things that never happened, and I don't think I should get into a car with you." He leans in and whispers, "Stranger danger."

Vance doesn't take Asher's shit. "Glad we agree and are being mature and a great friend and teammate."

Asher frowns, and I laugh. Hard.

"You're going to have to teach me that trick," I tell Vance.

"As long as you teach me how to turn off your stubbornness."

"I've heard blowjobs are great," Asher says, and I want to absolutely kill him.

Vance stands tall and folds his arms. "Seriously, how are you two friends? On one hand, I have Quinn, who says something innocent and then blushes because he thinks he crossed a line, and then there's you, just letting out whatever random sexual thing comes to mind without a care in the world."

Asher shrugs. "We're both queer in a male-dominated sport where people still fucking protest against pride night and some of our work colleagues refuse to wear pride jerseys. We're bonded through societal trauma."

"That's actually an insightful—" Vance starts.

Asher keeps talking. "Well, that, and I don't give a fuck what anyone thinks of me. Quinn is gross and cares about other people and their *feelings*."

"And then you finish with ... that." Vance shakes his head, and then his phone rings. "Hey, I'm just with Quinn and Dalton now. What's the plan?" He listens for a moment. Says, "Uh-huh." And then ends it with "See you soon." He glances at us. "Boone is meeting us at the clinic."

I don't want to go even more. If I don't get the scan, I technically haven't torn it. Right? Schrodinger's groin. It's both torn and not torn. That's a new take.

This sucks.

Not long later, I'm in a gown, getting scanned, poked, prodded at, and dreading every minute.

The worst part is the wait afterward. It takes. So. Fucking. Long.

"Good news," Dr. Travers says when he, Boone, and Vance walk back into my room. Dr. Travers has his offices near the practice rink, equipped with everything a sports doctor needs, like MRI machines, CAT scans, ultrasound, the works. Asher hasn't left my side and even got out of his weights session today, which is the only reason why I think he's still here. But then he reaches for my hand, bracing me for bad news, and I realize he's being big ol' softie Asher again.

I sit up in the bed. "It's not a tear?"

"Oh. Umm, I have ... news," Dr. Travers says.

Not going to lie. I'm pretty close to fucking crying. "How bad?" I hate that my voice breaks.

"That's the good news. It's a tiny, teeny, not even an eighth-of-an-inch tear. Completely healable with no medical intervention other than painkillers and rest. But when I say rest, I mean it. Not even getting up to get yourself a snack type of rest. Ideally, we'll have you bedridden completely for the first few days, and then after that, you can go to the bathroom and do necessary things, but nothing else."

Okay, so that's not the end of the world, but ... "How long for?"

And this is where it gets scary. Dr. Travers purses his lips. "Six weeks."

I slump against my pillow.

I'm out for six fucking weeks. "Six weeks in hockey is a lot of games that I'm going to miss."

"It's technically only five," Vance says. "All-Stars is coming up. You can stay on your couch and not move a muscle."

"And you'll be back before the end of the regular season," Boone says.

I hate this. I fucking hate this.

But not as much as Asher, apparently. "I have to be his babysitter for six weeks? What about away games? What about—"

"You won't have to look after him," Boone says. "Vance and I talked it out. He's going to take a break from away games and volunteered to stay with Quinn while O'Hennessy and I alternate road trips between us."

My gaze flies to Vance. "You're staying? With me?"

Just kill me now. End this nightmare once and for all.

CHAPTER EIGHT

VANCE

Did I take a knock to the head? Why did I volunteer to be the one to babysit Quinn? Knowing about his issues and how hard the news was going to hit him, though, made me want to be there for him. Sure, after a few weeks of constant care, it won't be so bad. I'll mostly be needed to check in a few times a day and drive him to any appointments he needs to go to.

These first few days though … I'll be with him basically full-time. It'd be easier to just move into his spare room, but that doesn't feel entirely ethical to me. All I'd be doing is sleeping in there, but with Quinn's crush and the way I feel about him, it'd seem like more than it is. So after spending the day working from his place and catering to his every whim, I'll then have to drive the half hour home again, only to be back here in time for him to wake up.

"What are you doing?" he asks as I push his coffee table aside.

"You complained about the couch nonstop last night. So I'm getting creative."

"Creat—"

I don't give him a chance to finish that question as I duck out of the room and head upstairs. My plan is to take his mattress to him for the next few days of rest, and I'm entirely unprepared for the awkwardness that hits the second I walk into his room.

It's so … personal.

His bed is unmade. One pillow on the floor, duvet crumbled by the foot of the bed. His open closet shows his clothes hanging neatly, with a pair of discarded pajama pants on the floor. It's exactly how he left it yesterday morning before training, and as I picture Quinn moving around his space, maybe stretching out his back or scratching that light blond trail of hair that runs down his lower abs … warmth passes through me.

Fucking hell.

I unstick my feet from the doorway and gather up his bedding. His scent is heavy on his sheets, but I ignore it as I carry the armful over to the stairs and throw it over the banister. Then I heft up the heavy mattress and drag it after me.

Quinn's looking way too amused by the time I get it downstairs.

"Shut up," I grunt.

"Didn't say anything."

I let the mattress fall onto the cleared space on the floor with a *thump*, then point to it. "You. Lie. Down."

"You know what? The couch is suddenly really comfy. I don't know what I was complaining about last night."

I laugh because there's no way he's not sleeping there now I've gone to all that effort. "Suddenly funny, are you?"

"I know it's hard to believe, but I have an actual personality when—" He cuts off, and I have a feeling I know where that sentence was going. It's almost tempting to just tell him I know how he feels and that it's not a big deal, but it obviously can't happen, no matter how much I might want it to. Then maybe he would relax around me.

Or maybe it would make everything a thousand times worse.

"Come on, I'll help you."

He sighs, resigned, and loops an arm around my shoulders as we shift him onto the floor. I grab his bedding and tuck him in, taking time to position his hips and legs properly.

"Cool, now all you have to do is lie there for about thirty-six hours. Easy."

"Easy," he deadpans.

"Hey, at least you're getting out of your away games this week."

"Right. Just what every hockey player wants. Not to play."

I resist pointing out this could have been so much worse and it's all his fault. "Ah. We're back to sulking Quinn."

"It's not like this is an easy time for me."

"Maybe not, but you're determined to make it harder."

"It's not ... I *was* taking it seriously, okay? I'd think I know my limits better than other people."

I wave a hand over him. "Clearly."

"Aren't you, you know, supposed to be kind or something? Sympathetic?"

"Nope," I answer happily. "I'm supposed to get results. And if that means pointing out when you're saying dumb things, I'll do it."

"So much for being scared of me getting you fired."

"So much for being scared of me benching you."

So help me, he almost smiles. At least, his lips twitch before he covers his mouth with his hand and runs his fingers over his mustache. "You, uh. You said something about evening the field. Earlier. Before—"

"You blurted out something inappropriate that made you blush?"

And there's the blush again. "Right. That."

I throw myself on his couch on my stomach and prop my head on my hand. "I was gonna say that since I've seen you at your most vulnerable, I can try to return the favor. Ask me something. I'll be honest."

Instead of relaxing him, Quinn's eyes shoot wide. "A-anything?"

"Anything appropriate for a player to ask their athletic trainer."

"Yeah, of course. Obviously."

I wait him out, and it's like I can see his mind racing.

"I ... I've got nothing."

"Nothing?"

He shakes his head.

"*Wow.*" I roll onto my back, dramatically clutching my chest. "So much interest. So much connection. It hurts."

"Dramatic much? What do you want to know about me?"

"Middle name."

His perplexed look is adorable. "Seriously?"

"Yeah. Shoot."

"Richard." He pulls a face. "My parents claim they don't hate me, but they named me Ayri Dick. Who does that?"

Once again, I have to remind myself not to laugh. "It, uh, has a ring to it."

"I used to get called fairy dick in high school."

"Oh."

He waves a hand. "It was mostly from friends, so it's fine. I know they weren't being mean, but they also didn't know I'm gay, and so it hit differently than what they meant."

My amusement dries up. "I'm sorry."

"Why? You gonna start calling me fairy dick?"

"No, because it's supposed to be me being vulnerable, not you again."

"Yeah, what the hell, man?" He throws a pillow at me, and I catch it and tuck it under my head.

"Need anything?"

"A new babysitter."

"Are you saying Dalton has a better bedside manner than me?"

"You're right. How did I get stuck with the two worst choices to ever choice?"

"Befriending Dalton was all on you. See what I mean about making your life harder?"

Before he can reply, his stomach growls loudly.

"Ah, fuck. I haven't fed you, have I?"

He hurries to grab his phone. "It's okay. I can order something."

"No way." I jump up from the couch. "You have food here?"

"Well, yeah, but …"

I snatch up the TV remote and put it on the music channel as I'm leaving the room, then drop the remote out of his reach.

"*Really*, Vance?" he yells after me.

"Lunch will be half an hour," I call back, then pretend I can't hear his grumbling over the sound of the music. Quinn reminds me of an only child who's used to getting what he wants while at the same time wanting approval from everyone around him. He's a bit … Naïve? Clueless? I can't exactly pinpoint this so-called personality he apparently locks away from me, but all that innocence is fun to tease. If I thought he actually had an issue with the music, I'd probably let him change it, but Quinn likes attention, and sulking gets him attention from me.

Which is definitely not something I should encourage.

It's also not something I can resist.

He's got chicken breast, a pantry full of spices, fresh salad, and a carton of eggs. I can work with this. I whistle to the music as I whip us up a Cajun chicken salad, then grab him a bottle of water and join him back in the living room. After I set everything on the table, I nudge his empty piss carton around the corner of the couch with my foot, then drop onto the mattress with him and place the tray I found between us.

"Enjoy."

His gaze travels from the plate to my face. "You can cook?"

"I grilled some chicken, calm down."

"That's cool."

"What, you can't? This is all your food."

"Yeah, but I stick to basic and easy."

"You have a pantry full of spices, and you don't use them?"

Quinn takes a bite and chews slowly. "Mom bought them last time she was in town. I wouldn't even know what half of them are."

"Lucky you have cooks and nutritionists on call if you need them."

He twists his lips. "In case you haven't noticed, I don't like asking for help."

"Shit. *Really?* No way ..."

"Shut up."

I shouldn't like teasing him as much as I do. "Yeah, it was *kinda* obvious that's a problem for you. But why?"

"My sister is older, so I was always the baby of the family. Throw in my baby face, and people underestimate me. They always assume I need to be helped or saved, and sometimes I want to prove I can do things for myself. I'm a fucking hockey player. I worked my ass off to get here. That's something *I* did."

"It's incredibly impressive."

"So what that I'm not some master-level chef. Most people can't stand up on ice, let alone shoot a tiny disk into a net."

"No disagreements from me."

"So, yeah. *That's* why I'm frustrating sometimes. Sorry, I guess. I don't know how to stop."

And there Quinn goes being vulnerable again. I don't think he can help it. He says he doesn't want to be saved or helped, and I get it, but he definitely wants to let people in. It's barely been a day, and I can tell he craves a support network. Sure, he has his Collective guys, but they're not in this city. It makes me think that's why he and Dalton got so close. Dalton needs people to rely on him, and Quinn needs someone he can rely on.

I'm starting to understand their friendship a whole lot more.

And learning these things about Quinn feels strangely indulgent.

"When I was in high school, this chick thought it would be funny to yank my shorts down in the middle of the quad. Only, I tend to free ball it more often than not, and the whole school got a good look at my butt. Called me Commando until I graduated."

Quinn's eyes are huge, and he looks torn between a laugh and sympathy.

I crack a smile. "Eh, I thought it was kinda cool. And I've got a big dick, so it was definitely good advertisement."

Quinn breaks down with laughter, one hand partially covering his reddening face. "Why am I not surprised that kind of thing wouldn't embarrass you?"

"I'm an easygoing guy."

"I've noticed." He stabs his fork at his salad. "So … you're like my servant for the next however long, huh?"

"At your beck and call."

"Damn. Makes me wish I had a pool now."

"Why? Would you dress me in a pool boy uniform and watch me work?"

"A uniform? I thought you went commando …"

"Dirty mind, Ayri Richard Quinn." I pretend to tsk.

His eyes are alive with laughter. "Do you know what Ayri means in Arabic?"

"No fucking clue."

He bites his lip like he's holding back a laugh. "It's … it means … dick."

"*Dick?*"

"Yup."

"So. Your parents. They named you—"

"Dick Dick Quinn. *Yeeep.*"

Now it's my turn to lose my shit laughing.

"And if you tell anyone that, I'll spread the commando story."

I pat his good leg. "Your secret is safe with me. Dick."

CHAPTER NINE

QUINN

"Okay, it's official," I say as Vance helps me back to the couch. I've been alternating between the couch and the mattress on the floor because lying in the one spot all day, every day, is making other body parts hurt.

"What is?"

"You've officially seen me at my worst. There's no reason to be embarrassed around you now because no matter what I do, it can't be as bad as you helping me to the bathroom."

"Hey, it was bound to happen eventually. I'm impressed you could hold it in for three days. The pee bottle wasn't going to handle that much crap."

I wish he wasn't talking literally. "You know what I've heard?"

Vance cocks his head with a damn smile on his face like this is nothing. "What did you hear?"

"Florida is looking for a new trainer. Maybe you should apply."

Vance laughs. "Trying to get rid of me when I've taken such good care of you?"

"Yes."

"How many times do I have to tell you I'm a health professional? Want to know where I did my placement in college for experience? Old people's home. At least with you, I only needed to help you on and off the toilet. Do you know how many old people I had to help out of their full diapers?"

"Good to know I'm one step above changing adult diapers."

"Hey, don't be so hard on yourself. You're at least two steps above that."

I throw my arm over my eyes. "If I can't see you, it means you're not here, right?"

Vance sits in my armchair across from me. "And I thought we were getting over this stage."

I uncover my face and stare at him. "What stage?"

"Where you're all nervous and squirrelly around me. I know it's not the real you. I've seen the real you with Dalton. With the rest of the team. You're only like this around me." Vance eyes me, like really eyes me, as if he's baiting me to admit how I feel.

Okay, I'm back on the he overheard bandwagon. "It's … and the … uh … buh, ma … Fucking hell." I can't admit it. I just can't.

"Hmm, we're going backward. Do you need more embarrassing stories about me? Let's see …" He taps his chin.

"Come on. You have to *think* about it? Have you always been all suave and put together? Awkward teen years? Give me something, please."

"My mom once caught me jerking off."

"Doesn't that happen to everyone at some stage? Next."

Vance huffs. "I already told you the pantsing story."

"Oh, how I wish I got through life with only those two minor memories of trauma to get me through," I deadpan.

"All right, here's something for you." He leans forward, placing his hands on his knees. "For the longest time, I thought women—all women—got their period on the same day. Like, as a collective hive with some queen. First of the month. Every month. I swear, learning all about anatomy in college was eye-opening."

Okay, that's kinda funny.

"Oh, I also thought they could, like, turn it on and off. Like if they had a date or whatever, they could hold it in until afterward."

I smile. "See, this is the stuff that makes me feel better about myself. Sure, I worry about how many times you've told me you're a health professional, but at least you know all about a woman's reproductive system now. Uh, right?"

"Shit, don't quiz me on it or anything, but yes, I lived a very sheltered life. I didn't have a mom or sister to teach me that stuff. It was just my dad and me growing up, and honestly, the education system is failing students in the sex education department."

"Sure. That's the problem. Could it maybe have been that whenever girl parts were mentioned, you tuned out because you've never had an interest in them?"

"Possibly," he murmurs. "We good now? Will you take my secret to the grave?"

"I have to, don't I? You've got dirt on me. A lot of dirt."

"What's friendship without a little blackmail?"

My eyes meet his. "Is that what we have? Friendship?"

Our eyes meet, and the way his gaze softens heats me to my core. I swear he's two seconds away from admitting we're friends or could be friends, or he wants to be friends, but he doesn't.

He waves me off. "Slip of the tongue. We're work … acquaintances?"

All those incel guys complain about being friend zoned. I just got acquaintance zoned.

Do I win loser of the year yet?

—

"You set for the night?" Vance asks as he comes back in the living room from doing the dishes after dinner.

"Think so."

"Last day of having me tomorrow. Then the team is back, and you can deal with Dalton for All-Stars week."

"Yaaaay," I deadpan.

"Would you rather I do it? I can. I'm the only single, unmarried trainer we've got."

Only gay one too, which is a shame. Why can't I have a crush on one of the others? It's so much easier to ignore those urges when they're straight.

And even though I'm still thinking of Vance in that sexual way, the easy back-and-forth is coming more naturally. "Ah, so that's the real reason Boone assigned you to me. Because you have no life." I smirk.

Vance laughs. "Wait, I don't think that's supposed to be funny."

"Is this one of those if you don't laugh, you'll cry moments?"

"Probably. I'm not going to think about it too hard, but the offer is there if you need me."

No, I would like a break from having Vance wait on me hand and foot, help me up and down off the stupid floor or couch, and definitely from having to empty my makeshift bedpan.

"It will be good for Asher to learn some humility," I say.

"Damn. I almost wish I was going to be here to see him doing half the stuff I've done for you these last few days."

"If you were here, he'd make you keep doing them."

"I don't doubt that for a second. Call me if you need anything."

"Will do."

Vance picks up his bag and heads for the door. It's like he's moving in slow motion, and for a brief, really brief second, I try to convince myself it's because he doesn't actually want to leave. But ... that can't be right.

Nope. It can't.

When he leaves, the door closing snaps my brain back into reality mode.

Work acquaintance. Work acquaintance. Work acquaintance.

There's a buzz from somewhere, but when I pick up my phone, it's not that. Sitting up, I glance around and find Vance's phone still on my coffee table.

I pull up his number to call him to come get it, but it occurs to me right at the last second that he obviously won't get the message when his phone is right here.

If I can get up and get to the door, I might be able to stop him before he pulls out of my driveway.

Getting there in time is another question because even though the pain in my leg is dimming every day, I'm still not supposed to use it. I've been relying on Vance to get me to and from everywhere, so even pulling myself into a standing position is difficult when I can't put weight on my left leg.

By the time I do manage to do it and hobble to the foyer, I'm panting, sweating, and I'm ready to collapse.

He's probably gone by now, and this will all have been a waste, but then my front door swings open, and Vance charges through like a bull in a china shop. "Sorry, I left my—*oomph*—"

We collide because he's not watching where he's going and doesn't realize I'm upright, which, in his defense, I shouldn't be.

"Oh, fuck," he lets out as we go down.

Somehow, he manages to spin us midair so I don't land on my leg—I'm assuming—but all that does is make me fall on top of *him*.

He grunts, and I hiss in pain, but when our eyes meet, something passes between us. I don't know what, but it's *something*.

Suddenly, the ache in my leg doesn't exist. Neither does the ability to breathe. All there is, is him and me and what I'm assuming—but not hoping—is his belt buckle hard between us.

I lick my lips instinctively and then hate myself for it, but in the next moment, he's mimicking the action.

"Phone," he croaks.

I blink out of my Vance trance. Hey, that rhymes. "What?"

"I forgot my phone." His voice is even raspier.

"I know. That's why I got up when I wasn't supposed to."

His lips quirk. "Good to know. I was thinking you might have been partying every night I left the house. Maybe you do need a babysitter."

I huff. "Please, I'm not Oskar Voyjik."

Vance's laughter makes both our bodies shake, and that's when I realize I'm still on top of him.

"Sorry. I'll—" I try to move, but he pulls me close and holds me to him.

There's that moment again. That crackle of energy— chemistry—firing between us.

He lifts his head off the floor, his mouth moving closer. Closer.

My eyes shut slowly, my lips quivering in anticipation of his mouth on mine. I swear I can feel his breath on my skin. It makes me light-headed, picturing the exact moment his mouth will brush mine.

But then he says, "Are you okay?" and the spell is broken.

When I open my eyes again, his head is back on the floor, and I have to wonder if I imagined him moving at all.

I scramble off him, careful of my leg. "I am. Well, I don't think I did any more damage. Put it that way."

He clears his throat. "Uh. Good. That's good. I'm just going to …" He nods toward the coffee table, where his phone is, gets to his feet, and then pockets his cell. "Need help getting back to the mattress?"

The Vance I've dealt with the last three days wouldn't have given me the choice, so I look at him, perplexed by his question.

"I should go. I'm late. I'm running … uh, late. Okay, bye. Again. See ya." He moves around me—literally has to walk around where I'm on my ass in the middle of my foyer—and leaves again.

While I remain still, trying to catch up with what the fuck just happened.

I'm still sitting here a minute later when the door opens again.

My heart skips a beat, thinking he's come back for a second time, but no dice.

In the doorway stands Asher fucking Dalton and his gorgeous, blond boyfriend, Kole.

"Happy All-Stars week! I brought you reinforcements." He gestures to Kole. "He's premed, so he can look after your boo-boos while the others from the Collective come here and drink away All-Stars weekend."

"Here? They're coming here?" The place is a mess, and I have nothing to feed them, and—

78

"Relax. I've handled everything."

Beside him, Kole sighs. "And by him, he means me. Groceries are on their way, I can clean, help you shower, and get into fresh clothes—"

"No you fucking won't," Asher says.

"No I won't, what?"

"You're not showering with Ayri Quinn."

You know Asher's serious when he uses my full name. Or my first name in general.

"I'm not showering with him. I'm helping him shower," Kole argues. "*Look* at him. He's in the middle of his floor by himself. He obviously can't stand on his own."

Which reminds me. "Speaking of which, can either or both of you help me up?"

They grab an arm each and pull me up to my feet but don't stop arguing.

"I've seen his dick a million times in the locker room," Asher says. "I'll do it."

Kole tries to look disappointed, but I can totally see his smile of victory. "If you insist."

Kole lets me go and heads for the kitchen.

I laugh. "I think you just got played."

Asher grunts. "So do I, but I stand by my decision. He doesn't get to check out any of my teammates naked. End of story."

They're so cute.

I wish I had someone I could be with like that.

Maybe someone who's not off-limits and is emotionally available. Is that so much to ask?

I could've sworn Vance was about to kiss me, but I guess that shows just how naïve I am when it comes to guys.

Dating, love, and relationships are impossible to work out when you're completely clueless.

CHAPTER TEN

VANCE

I've learned two things about myself this morning.

First, I'm not as professional as I think I am.

Second, I like the feel of Ayri Quinn pressed up against me way too much.

I can't believe I almost kissed him. Right there in the entryway. Sore leg be damned. And given how I passed Dalton on the way out of there, we definitely would have been caught.

When did I get this stupid? Because it takes an epic level of stupidity to cross lines with a player.

The sight of Quinn with his eyes closed and lips parted plays behind my eyes. It was such a hot fucking view. I wanted to feel his mustache scrape my lip as I pressed my tongue into his mouth.

And according to how my cock hasn't waned, I still do. This is bad.

I've never, ever been attracted to a player before, and while I've always known that Quinn is hot, that he's powerful on the ice, and cute as heck when he stumbles out a sentence, I've always been able to keep that side of me in control.

The side of me that shouldn't exist.

It has to be that he's queer. He's gay and available and wants me. It's all a circumstance-y, proximity thing, right? Isn't that how it goes? Like a last-man-on-Earth scenario?

I ignore that I've worked on Dalton before and have less than zero desire to kiss *him*. He'd probably bite my face off.

No, Quinn's the one my dick is after, and the damn thing is getting demanding about it.

Which means there's only one thing I can do.

Since the team got back today, the practice facilities are quiet, with the occasional player sneaking in a light skate or some rehab work. Boone is in his office like I thought he'd be, probably reading through the reports I was working on while he was away. The bulk of our job is hands-on, but everything needs the paperwork behind it to cover our asses.

Boone smiles as soon as he spots me. "Hey, hey. How's the babysitting going?"

Is he a fucking mind reader? I pull a face and drop into the chair opposite him. Boone's technically my boss, but he's not one of those guys who lords the position over us. He trusts us to do our job and only follows up if we've fucked up somewhere.

And I've definitely fucked up.

"I ... can't do it anymore."

"What? Why?"

This really, *really* isn't a conversation I want to be having, so I just blurt it out. "I've been having inappropriate thoughts about Quinn, so I think I need to put some distance between us."

Boone stares at me for a moment before switching his computer screen to sleep. "Has anything happened?"

"No."

He pins me in place with his dark eyes. "Anything at all? Something that could be misinterpreted by Quinn, or—"

"No, nothing. I've only ever been professional, and I intend to stay that way. I'm only telling you because I know you trust us, and I think it'd be better if you or O'Hennessy covered things with his care, and I'll get a home nurse lined up until he's back."

"Okay. Thank you for being up-front."

"Of course."

"Does he know about any of this?"

I'm about to shake my head but pause. "I overheard him talking to Dalton in the locker room the other day. About having a crush on me."

Boone rubs his temple. "Well, this is complicated."

"Yep. Especially since I find him hot as hell."

"Is Quinn attractive in gay circles? Even with that porn star stache he's got going on?"

I think of how that "porn star stache" would feel scraping over my dick. "It has its advantages, yeah."

He holds up a hand, on the verge of laughter. "Don't need to know more."

"As fun as it is to squick you out, what do we do here?"

"There's technically no protocol, so I guess we just need to make it up as we go along. Power imbalances aside, I don't need to tell you that failed relationships can fuck with a team, which is why management frowns on that kind of thing."

"Agreed."

"So I guess, well, what's the end goal? He's got a crush, and you … what?"

"I barely know him, so a relationship isn't even on my radar. It's purely, uh, *physical.*" Which is kind of a bullshit lie the more I think about it. The last few days with Quinn have warmed me to him on a whole other level. Seeing him start to relax—even if only a little—has been fun, and I've learned more about him than I would have thought I could.

"I'm not going to mince words here. It's my preference that you don't pursue whatever it is. A hookup might be fun at the time, but if he wants more and you don't, or the other way around, it'll be a terrible working environment for all of us. That said, I can't expressly stop you. Management can't either. But they *can* trade him if they get worried about brand damage. Fuck, the guy has a groin injury. We both know where your hands have been, and if he claims foul play—"

"He wouldn't."

"I don't get that vibe from him either, but you can very easily see how people could claim an abuse of power."

"Yeah, I get that."

"I think being taken off his care team is the right call. Whether or not something does happen, it's the safest option."

"Agreed."

He studies me for a moment. "You okay?"

A loud exhale rushes from me. "It's just a bit frustrating that a guy I'm interested in is actually interested in return and it can't go anywhere."

He shrugs. "Well, that part is up to you. But I don't think I need to remind you that there are a whole lot of other guys out there who'd be happy to date you. You know. If you ever left work."

I give him a sheepish smile. "Point taken."

"Uh-huh."

"Thanks for listening. And not being a dick about it."

"You're a grown man. Your life is yours to fuck up if that's the path you want to take."

"So motivational."

"You know it."

I leave Boone to it and head into the treatment rooms. With Quinn at home and most of the players resting from their away game, it's a quiet afternoon. O'Hennessy has earned his afternoon off, and while I put in more hours than I should have with Quinn, I wasn't technically supposed to be there from morning until night. I just ... *was*.

At least his days of being completely stationary are all but over. I'll give Dalton some crutches to take to Quinn, because my time with him is done. Even though I know

I've made the right decision, I still feel like shit when I pick up the phone and make a call to a home nurse service.

It's what we should have done in the first place, if I'm honest, but I'd *wanted* to be the one there for him.

All I achieved was being hit hard by temptation, and now I need it to go away again.

Crushes pass, and if I give Quinn the time he needs, his will as well. It'll be easier for me to get back professional control when I shouldn't see him for three to five weeks, depending on his recovery.

It'll give me enough time to get my head back on properly too.

A few weeks.

Then everything will be back to normal.

-

Since Boone seems to think I do nothing but work, I text my friend Joe to meet up the next night. We went through college together and try to catch up once a month. He's got a young family, which makes it hard, but I'm *not* a workaholic, fuck you very much, Boone. I can catch up with friends.

Joe's already waiting at a bar table with two beers in front of him. The sports bar is loud, with the All-Stars skills night playing on the overhead televisions. I take the seat opposite him.

"You know, I told myself by catching up that it proves all I do isn't work, but ..." I wave at all the hockey going on. "I'm not sure that's entirely true."

"Any Buffalo players up there?"

"Our goalie."

"Then you're good. Just enjoy the skills tests."

"That, I can do." I tip my beer his way and take a long sip. It's nice to get out and loosen up. Get my head off Quinn.

"What's new with you?" he asks.

"Not a lot. Just spent the week babysitting an injured player and nearly kissed him." I send a crooked smile Joe's way. "Nothing special."

"*What?* Dude! Tell me you're joking?"

"I'm joking?"

"Fuck me." He runs a hand over his face. "What is wrong with you?"

"Should we start a list?"

"You can't get involved with a player."

"Relax. I told my boss what happened, and we both agreed it would be better I don't work one-on-one with him anymore."

"Good." Joe eyes me over his beer. "Wait. If it's all organized, why are you bringing it up?"

"No reason."

His face slowly sets with disapproval. "Tell me you're not thinking about what I think you're thinking about."

"If I followed that, I probably would."

"You can't sleep with a player."

I know what he's saying, and I totally agree with him. But there's one giant *but* to that sentence.

I really, really want to.

"Hear me out."

"No."

I toss a coaster at him. "I'm not technically working with him anymore."

"Vance, you can't."

"Yeah, I *know* that. But if I do …"

"Ethically, that is so wrong."

Okay, now I'm starting to get annoyed. "Why is it? He has a thing for me, I'm not treating him anymore, nothing has happened so far, and it probably won't, but I'm just saying *if* it does … is that so bad?"

"Yes."

"Why?"

"Because he's your client."

"Not anymore."

"I … I …"

"Yeah, you don't have a reason, do you?"

"Just keep it in your pants, Vance."

I laugh because I'm easily amused. It's not like I *want* to pursue a serious thing with Quinn. I'd prefer just about anything else, if I'm honest. I'm not into complicated, and I'm going to use the next weeks of separation to move on, but if I can't? Yeah, I don't trust myself to be a strong-willed guy. It's pathetic how easily I fall for a pretty face, and Quinn? Hot damn, he's pretty.

Gorgeous eyes, strong jaw, soft cheeks, and that mustache that makes him look older. Then there's the way he blushes, and his strong hairy thighs, and how he laughs when he forgets to be self-conscious …

"You're thinking about him, aren't you?" Joe asks.

"Sure am."

"Man, you are so fucked."

"Eh, we'll see. We nearly kissed *yesterday*. Let me get a bit of distance."

"Just do me a favor and don't tell me when it happens. I'd like to trick myself into thinking I still have respect for you."

I grin. "At least one of us does. I lost respect for myself a long time ago."

CHAPTER ELEVEN

QUINN

I hate that I can't get that almost-maybe-kiss out of my head. I could've sworn we were *this* close, and then Vance backed off. He probably thinks I'm obsessed with him or something when I'm not.

I'm not.

Yet, with every new detail I learn about him, the more I find him irresistibly sexy. Even his lack of knowledge when it comes to female anatomy is somehow charming. It's going to make it that much harder to face him when he comes over to check on me this morning.

When my doorbell rings and my heart jumps into my throat, it's almost like the universe's way of saying, "Not obsessed, my ass."

The Queer Collective invaded Buffalo last night, and we had an All-Stars viewing party. Tradition. Apparently. But they all went to their respective hotels or, in Asher and Kole's case, home, so no one's here to get the door for me, and while technically, I'm allowed to be up and about today, I'll wait until Vance gives me the all clear.

Him ringing the doorbell must be a test. "It's open," I call out while my heart kicks up a notch.

I hope our near miss doesn't make shit awkward—more awkward—between us, but with the way the door slowly creaks and he takes his time coming inside, I fear that's exactly what I've gone and done.

I've made him uncomfortable by making a pass at him, even though it wasn't so much a conscious thing. I was sucked into the moment, misread the situation, and fucked up.

How much I fucked up doesn't become obvious until O'Hennessy turns the corner and smiles.

"Oh, hey." It's impossible to school my surprise.

"Vance had stuff to do today, so Boone sent me."

I don't know what to say to that.

"How are we doing this morning?"

"All right. I would love to take a piss though."

"I'll help you to the bathroom. The game plan was to get you up and moving about today, right?"

"Supposed to be, but I had a fall yesterday—"

He does a double take. "Fall? What were you doing up?"

Trying to hump your coworker.

"Bathroom," I lie.

"Where was Vance?"

"Uh, he'd already left."

"Okay, here's what we'll do ..." O'Hennessy says. "We'll get you to the bathroom, and then I'll check you over once we're back."

I reach for my piss bottle. "Vance had me going in this if you want to check me over without moving me."

O'Hennessy laughs. "Damn, what a tyrant. You're fine to move to the bathroom so long as you're not putting any weight on your leg."

"Why couldn't you have been the one to look after me for the last three days?"

"What I don't understand is why it's taken them this long to hire you a home nurse."

"A what?"

"Starting tomorrow, you'll get daily visits from an actual nurse instead of having one of us annoying you."

My mood takes a nosedive because … that means Vance isn't coming back?

That's it?

No explanation, no nothing. Just … gone.

Well, doesn't that make me feel like the sexiest man alive? I creeped him out so much he decided to never come back.

O'Hennessy helps me to the bathroom and back and then gets me down on the ground to stretch out my leg. It's the first time I've been allowed to try to do anything with it, even though it hasn't been feeling too bad. And of course, because I'm me, and because I was the idiot who went dancing, it really fucking hurts at the slightest pressure.

"Damn," O'Hennessy says.

"Yup."

"How'd you fuck it up so badly? Vance said something about running?"

I let out a relieved breath. If it didn't scare him off so much, I'd offer to kiss Vance for lying for me.

"Yeah," I say softly.

"Rotten luck. You must've just overworked it that little bit too hard while you were still recovering from the strain."

Yes. Luck. All luck's fault. Not stubbornness at all.

Totally.

"Your range of motion isn't great."

"No shit."

He ignores me. "But your pain is confined to anything past regular movements, so I'd say you're fine to move around if you have to, but ice and rest is still what's best for it."

"So I don't need Dalton to help me to the bathroom tonight?"

"Tonight? What's happening tonight?"

"All-Stars gathering with some of the other queer players. They all came here because I can't move."

"Oh, that's nice of them."

"You'd think that, but no. I've spent most of my time trying to get Dalton to shut his mouth about my—and I quote—'broken dick.'"

O'Hennessy chuckles. "With friends like him, eh?"

"I'm a lucky guy." And while I say it dryly, I'm only half-joking.

"Okay, rest up, and tomorrow, your nurse will be coming by to check on you, to help you up and get around the place. You only need to focus on healing that leg, got it?"

"Got it."

"Anything else you need before I go?"

"Nope."

But as he packs up his stuff and heads for the door, I can't help myself.

"Why did they hire a nurse now instead of days ago?"

"I think Boone needed Vance back on deck after he had to go on a road trip. The dreaded road trips."

Being head of the athletic department, Boone does his fair share of road trips, but it is usually Vance that's there when we're away. I guess like he said, he's single, without a family or kids. If I were the boss, I'd send him on as many as I possibly could too.

Still, one little road trip wouldn't have sent Boone into a spiral that he'd have to pull Vance back. Especially when it's All-Stars week. Sure, the team still has practices and weight schedules—it's not a completely free week off— but we do have more time on our hands than we usually do during the regular season. We get a break for once.

And even though I try to tell myself that Vance maybe just wanted his break, I know, deep down, it's because I tried to kiss him.

Why am I the way that I am?

—

It turns out I might not be the only clueless moron in this group. You'd think that would make me feel better, but it doesn't. We're all just dumbasses here.

Aleks is dating this new guy, a hot firefighter guy, and he's freaking out because of babies? Or not having babies. It's something about babies. I'm only half listening because I'm stuck on how to fix this Vance situation.

Obviously, I need to apologize, but how the fuck do I do that without making it worse? More uncomfortable. Or maybe we're at rock bottom, so the only place we can go from here is up.

"Hey, Oskar?" I interrupt whatever they're talking about now.

"Yes, thing on Quinn's face that's getting way out of control?"

More stache jokes. Love it. Actually, I still prefer that over baby cheeks. "How did you and Lane become … you and Lane? Like, was there a weird moment between you two, and then it was awkward, and then—"

"Whoa, you had a weird moment with Vance?" Asher asks.

"What? No. I'm just curious. Because of the whole Lane getting fired for being with Oskar, and the power imbalance, and, and, and—"

"You totally had a moment with Vance!"

"Who's Vance?" Oskar asks.

"Their team trainer," Aleks supplies for me. Damn him. He was there the first time I was injured, playing against us.

A round of "Oooh" breaks out.

"Nothing happened," I say. "But I thought something might have, but I was wrong because he ran out of here

95

like his ass was on fire, and then this morning, he sent O'Hennessy to do his job for him. I think I crossed a line, and I don't know how to say sorry without making it worse." I turn to Oskar. "I'm just assuming the beginning of your relationship was full of you apologizing a lot."

Everyone laughs, but I'm being serious. If anything, Lane has toned Oskar down *a lot*.

"Pfft. You never have to apologize if you never do anything wrong."

Toned down. Not given him a lobotomy. Obviously.

"Next time you see him, insult him," Ezra says. "That's how I won this one over." He points to Anton.

Anton looks completely serious when he says, "Yes. That is definitely the thing that made me fall for him and not hate him for a good ten years beforehand."

"Exactly." Ezra nods.

"I think you should ignore him," Asher says. "Play hard to get and show no emotions."

"He could just talk to the guy," Foster, who plays for Montreal, adds. "You know, communication and all that."

Everyone in the room screws up their face at Foster.

Ezra shakes his head. "Don't listen to that advice. Sounds healthy, and that's a trap."

"That kinda makes me want to do it more. Going against the grain here is probably the smartest thing to do."

Foster leans forward on his seat. "Plus, I probably have the most healthy relationship here."

We all glance around at each other.

Anton shrugs. "Hate to say it, but it's true."

Oskar looks like he tasted something sour. "Eww. Emotionally stable people."

There are rounds of agreements, but Foster just raises his beer in the air and then takes a sip, sending a wink my way.

Okay. Grown-up talk.

Apologize for crossing the line.

Move on.

Can totally do it.

Yup.

Definitely.

CHAPTER TWELVE

VANCE

> **Quinn:**
> I've fallen and can't get up. Help!

You've got to be kidding me. Only a few days of light movement and he's already fucked up. Why is he so goddamn stubborn? I sigh as I merge into a turning lane and head back the way I've just come. Thankfully, Quinn doesn't live far from the arena, so it isn't a massive detour.

The whole way to his house, I work myself up, cursing him out for not caring about the team or himself. When we last spoke, I got the impression he was planning to take his rehab seriously, but if he can't get up himself ... what the hell has he done?

I swear, if he's made his injury worse, no more lying for him. I'll tell everyone he reinjured himself grinding up against some guy on the dance floor.

It'll serve him right.

I'm too busy being pissy at him that I forget to fixate on the fact I'm about to be face-to-face with the guy I need distance from since our kinda almost-kiss. But when I pull up out the front and see Quinn sitting on a love seat on his porch, my stomach flips out at the sight of him.

A couple of days was *not* long enough to stop him from taking over my system.

Thankfully, it looks like Dalton or someone has been keeping the path clear of snow, so I follow it up and pause at the base of his stairs. His cheeks are red, knitted hat pulled down over his ears, and he looks cuddly in an oversized coat, sweats, and fluffy socks. The ache to touch him hits hard.

"So you got back up," I say.

Quinn puffs a breath. "I didn't fall down."

"You …" My gaze strays from the crutches propped against the wall beside him to his strapped leg. "Then what's with the message?"

"You can thank Asher for that."

"What does Dalton have to do with anything?"

His pretty eyes flick away as he scuffs the socked toes of his good foot against the porch. "I might have been trying to text you. To talk. And apparently, I was being a big baby, so he took my phone and did the job for me. Then he ran off before he had to face you."

I laugh. "And he called *you* a baby."

I take the two steps up and sit beside him. It's freezing, but my coat helps, and there's something I like about the chill that fills my lungs every time I breathe in.

"You wanted to talk to me?"

He grimaces. "I was hoping you missed that part."

"Sorry to disappoint. But I'm here now, so might as well get it over with."

"Why did you send O'Hennessy? And book a nurse?"

Holy shit, he actually sounds … disappointed. I'd be lying if I said it didn't hurt. The thing is, I thought I could get away with being a coward about this whole thing. No way in hell did I imagine Quinn would ask me outright, considering how he couldn't manage a sentence around me before.

And since I never thought he'd ask, I have no clue how to answer.

"I have a team too, and I couldn't leave them to do everything."

"The nurse comes twice a day. You couldn't have managed that on the way to and from work?"

"I'm not your babysitter."

"No, but you volunteered to be."

I fight the urge to run away from this conversation.

Quinn drags in a long, loud breath, then whispers, "Is it because I tried to kiss you?"

"*What?*" I spin toward him so fast he actually meets my eyes. "I'm the one who almost kissed *you*."

"You … you what?"

"Fuck. I'm sorry. It was so, so *wildly* inappropriate. The last thing I want you thinking is that I tried to take advantage of you or whatever, but you were on top of me, and you're a good-looking guy who has a crush on me—I didn't exactly stop to think of logistics."

"I'm … wait," he says breathlessly. "You *know*?"

"About the crush?" I look away. "Yeah, I heard you and Dalton talking."

"I *knew* it."

I smile at how panicked he sounds, wanting to desperately tell him I feel the same but knowing once it's out there, everything will be so much harder. "Relax. In case you couldn't tell, I'm flattered."

"Oh my God." He buries his face in his hands, but even that isn't enough to hide how red his ears have gone.

"Don't worry, after everything you now know about me, I'm assuming that crush is long gone." I don't know why—actually, that's a lie. I know exactly why I said that. I want Quinn to deny it. Because I'm a sad, sexually frustrated man. But instead of a denial, all Quinn does is let out a squeak.

"Ah, we're back to communicating in random noises, are we? In that case, *oh la ka boo*."

He snorts, finally letting his hands drop. "Okay. It's official. Crush gone."

"Damn, really? Because those noises do it for me."

His face is still flaming, but he manages to talk, at least. "You're really not ... I didn't make you uncomfortable?"

"Are you serious? I followed you to that shithole of a bar after I found out how you felt about me. If I were uncomfortable, would I have been there?"

"But you were just trying to do your job, and every time you do that, I tend to shove my dick in your face." He shudders. "Even thinking about it makes me feel skeevy and pervy and gross."

That makes me laugh. "You can't help what your dick does. It's your middle name."

"And first. I was doomed from the start."

"True. Want me to help you back inside?"

"Soon."

I turn and prop my elbow on the two-seater bench. "Think I'm hanging around, do you?"

"Unless you're planning on forcing me to go back inside on my own." He gives me puppy dog eyes, and damn him, it works.

"You've got crutches."

"And you *said* you'd be here for me. Queer player, sticking together and all that."

I hang my head back dramatically. "Don't hold me to my word. That's a terrible quality to have."

"I'll let you put on the music channel," he sings, and that easiness he has with me—the very minuscule moments I've experienced so far—makes another appearance. It's a toss-up which I like better, the stammering or him being relaxed around me.

The way that I yearn for both tells me it's not a good idea for us to be alone together.

"You know I can't stay."

He frowns. "Why?"

"Because it's not professional."

So help me, he rolls his fucking eyes.

"Sure, grow a mustache to look more mature, but keep up the petulant teen attitude."

"Do I need to remind you that you're the one who followed me to a bar?"

Ooh, he's got me there. This new side of Quinn is fun and way too persuasive. "Unlike you, I'm not willing to risk my job."

"Low blow. All I'm asking is for you to hang out."

I chuckle. "You don't just 'hang out' alone with the guy you're into. It doesn't happen."

Quinn's forehead crumples sweetly. "Why?"

He's either ridiculously naïve or playing me because I'm not about to say *I'll end up throwing myself at you* out loud. If he thinks there's hope between us, he's not going to let the crush go, and so far, I'm not doing much of anything to convince him this can't happen.

Because I want it to happen.

His long, lean body right beside mine is tempting. Warm in the cool air. Those gorgeous hazel-gold eyes are looking right at me, and it would be all too easy to lean in and press my lips to his. I'm craving it. To feel his skin against mine.

His lips pull up. "You're looking at me funny."

I groan and swing back around to face the front. Quinn doesn't let me escape that easily though. He leans in, mist from his exhales meeting my cheek.

"Did you really want to kiss me?"

"Still do."

He sucks in a startled breath. "You do?"

"But I won't."

"Vance …" His raspy voice sticks on my name.

"Nuh-uh. Nope." I jump up from my place beside him and put distance between us. Leaning back against the banister gives me at least two feet of space to think clearly. Unlucky for me, Quinn has long legs, and he reaches out to cover my shoe with his socked foot.

"We'll just hang out. I'll be good."

Oomph. Just him calling himself "good" gives me some wicked ideas. "Stop that."

He blinks. "Stop what? I just said I'll behave."

I have to bite my knuckles. "I hate you."

"I really don't know what's happening."

"That just makes it worse." I hold back my laugh at his confused expression and grab his crutches for him.

"I thought you were going to help me."

"Yeah, no way am I risking touching you right now."

"Are you …" He drops his voice. "You know …"

"I am *you know.* Now, take these damn crutches and get in the house before you freeze. The last thing you need on top of your leg is pneumonia."

"Good point."

And even though I'm determined not to touch him, I stay close behind in case he needs me, trying—and failing—not to focus on the way his sweats hug his glorious ass. Given how good I'm being, I don't know why the universe is so determined to punish me.

"Need anything?" I ask as Quinn lowers slowly onto the couch.

"A massage?"

"Seriously?"

He pouts. "My leg hurts."

"Does it actually, or are you trying to get me to touch you?"

He laughs. "But if you touch me, maybe you'll try to kiss me again."

"*Ayri!*"

"What? If we both want it, I don't get why it can't happen."

I cross to take my usual seat on the coffee table. "I'm trying hard here to make things easier on us both. There might not be rules around us hooking up, but think about it. If we sleep together and one or both of us ends up pissed off at the other, how do you think the team will react? The coaches? Management? I could be fired, or you could be traded. If the media found out, who knows what kind of rumors they'd circulate."

His eyebrows knot. "What, like, inappropriate stuff?"

"I'm working on you. I babysat you for a few days in your house. While you were basically defenseless. When it comes to your injury, I have authority over you and your career. Don't you see how easily that could be manipulated?"

"I guess …"

"I'm sorry. Trust me, I'm interested. But one night together isn't worth all the what-ifs that could come after."

His whole body deflates, and he reaches up to slide the wool hat off his head, leaving his sweaty hair at all angles. Just like when he removes his helmet. He's so sweetly unkempt I have to slide my hands under my thighs to stop from raking them through his hair.

"Okay. I get it."

"I'm sorry," I say again.

"I know." He smiles. "Sucks I couldn't get one kiss though."

"Stop trying to tempt me."

"Do you blame me? All this time, I thought it'd never happen. Just let me enjoy knowing that you're not exactly immune to me either."

"Yes, yes, you're very hot and whatever."

"You too. Especially when your hands are right …" He lifts his foot again, gently sliding it along my inner thigh, and I let that cheeky shit get way higher than I should. He stops just before he reaches my dick and digs his toe into the fleshy part of my thigh. "Here. Gets me every time."

I hiss and catch his foot. "Had your fun yet?"

"No. Not even close." But he pulls his foot back anyway, and my cock hates it. It takes too long for me to release him, and when I do, I can't make myself stand up either.

"I'm not going to see you for a few weeks," I say.

"Okay."

"And when you're back at training, it's probably best we're not one-on-one either."

"Okay."

"At least … not if no one else is around." Because I've gotta leave a loophole in there somewhere, right? I hate myself.

"And if other people are around?" Of course he'd ask.

"We'll just see what happens."

"Okay."

"That's all you're going to say?"

Quinn shrugs. "As embarrassing as it is that you know, it's out there now. I want to climb you like a tree. You want me to climb you like a tree. There are a billion reasons why we shouldn't. I get it."

"Good thing your leg's out of commission and there'll be no climbing for you."

He doesn't answer me, and there's literally no other reason for me to stay.

Other than the fact I want to. To climb onto the couch beside him. To press my weight down against him. To feel his lips open for me. To strangle that messy hair in my grip.

Instead, I push to my feet.

"See you when you're back."

The small smile isn't the kind I like to see on his face. "Yeah. See you then."

CHAPTER THIRTEEN

QUINN

If Vance thinks a couple of weeks away from each other will do anything to squash my attraction to him, he obviously doesn't know how long I've been wanting to jump his bones.

Honestly, hearing if we weren't working together that he'd totally hook up with me has only made me more hard for him. Where I used to try to think of other things— porn, famous people, anyone but Vance—while jerking off, I now welcome his image. I fuck my fist nearly every night, reliving being on top of him, our almost-kiss. And when that doesn't do the job, I imagine what it would've been like to actually kiss him right there on my lobby floor. In the fantasy, I'm not injured, and kissing leads to sex where clothes only take a second to get rid of, and I don't need any prep for him to fuck me on the hardwood floors.

It's actually been a long three weeks when I think about it too hard.

Today, I'm finally back at practice, not cleared to play yet, but one of the team trainers has put time aside to test my leg with stretches, massage, and to go for a walk on the treadmill. Starting small, recovering big, and only kind of hoping Vance is on duty. I miss his big hands on me, and it's funny, but now that I know he wants to have sex with me too, my ill-timed boners don't feel like something I should be ashamed of. If anything, it could be a fun way to get Vance to make that same tortured face that he did on my porch.

Knowing I don't have to try and hide my crush or worry about freaking him out, has given me a new boost of confidence when it comes to him.

The longer I've had off, the more rejuvenated I am. My body is ready to get back into the game, even though I know it will be a slow process to get back to where I was. The other thing I've managed to gain perspective on is just how close I came to kissing my career goodbye.

If it had been a large tear or had separated from the joint, I wouldn't be here, walking the halls of the practice rink, trying to get back to physical peak so I can dominate on the ice.

I'd be drowning my sorrows and wondering what to do with my life.

I can't get that close to losing everything again. So no more bullshit. No more pushing. If I'm in pain, I'll speak up, and I'll get my season back on track. Thanks to Asher and his killer rookie season and the fact our team has synced for the first time in decades, we're having a great year. While my time off has been significant, if we make it to the playoffs, I can prove my worth again. I can show them I'm indispensable.

I get to the treatment room, and my heart sinks when only Boone is in there.

He turns and smiles. "Strip, and up you get. Let me check you over."

I do as he says, and he starts on my thigh, working the muscles in my quads and checking for any sore spots.

"How has recovery been?"

"Good. I followed instructions by the book and haven't done anything for three weeks."

"I bet you're itching to get back out on the ice."

"Fuck yes."

Boone's eyes widen.

"Sorry. I've been going a bit stir-crazy with nothing to do all day. I want back out there."

"But not before you're ready this time, right?"

I nod. "Right."

"It's a hard lesson for you athletes to learn, and you're lucky you didn't write off your whole season."

"I know, I know. You can spare me the lecture. Hockey is everything to me, and I was terrified I'd get sent back down to the farm team if I showed weakness, so I convinced myself I had to be fine when I wasn't."

"And now?"

"Now I've had a hard dose of reality and realize I could've lost more than my spot in the NHL. I could've lost it all."

Boone works his way up my leg and into the adductor where the sprain and small tear were. It's still tender, and I wince, but it's nothing compared to the pain I've experienced since the initial injury.

"Feels good," Boone says. "A little tight, but good."

From somewhere behind us, there's a crash that echoes around the small room.

I crane my head around, and Vance is there, hastily picking up the boxes of tape that he'd dropped. It sends a thrill through me to see him again and to see him so flustered at the words *tight* and *feels good*, even though there's nothing sexual about it. With Boone and O'Hennessy, it's always been easy to only hear professional speak. Never with Vance though, and now he's getting a taste of his own medicine.

My attention goes back to the ceiling above me while Boone continues to work on me, and I can't be blamed for what comes out of my mouth next. "Mm, that spot right there."

"Sore?"

"Nah, just more tightness. It's so *stiff*." I have to bite my lip to stop from laughing.

I can't be sure, but I swear Boone is holding back a smile too.

"I'm going to take my break." Vance rushes out of the room.

"Proud of yourself?" Boone asks.

My face falls. "Huh?"

"He told me. About you two ..."

I swallow hard. "What do you mean?"

"That spending time together might have brought up inappropriate feelings for each other."

I don't say that I've had those inappropriate feelings for a hell of a lot longer. "He ... told you that?"

"He wanted me to know why he couldn't work with you anymore."

"Oh," I murmur. If he told his boss about it, then he's definitely serious that nothing can happen. All the hope I'd been holding on to withers inside me.

"I can't tell two grown-ass adults what to do, but before any lines get crossed, you should both think of the team first."

"Don't worry. He's determined to remain professional."

Boone laughs. "Like telling a man what he can't have isn't going to make him want it more."

"I promise we won't let anything interfere with the team, and I won't do anything at all if it threatens his position here." I mean that. Truly. Being responsible for someone getting fired would kill me.

"Good. You're all done." Boone pulls his hands away. "I want you on the treadmill and to go until your leg starts to hurt, and I don't mean excruciating, can no longer go on kind of pain. I mean, the tiniest little tweak. A single spark of something. Anything. You stop and cool down. Got it?"

"Got it."

"When you get back to running for thirty minutes without pain, that's when I'll let you back on the ice."

I light up inside. "For games?"

"For practice. Don't rush this, Quinn."

"You're right. Sorry. I'm just excited to get back out there."

Why was I excited to get back out here again?

It's literally my first game back. I've played the long game—weeks of working up my times on the treadmill, stopping anytime something felt the slightest bit *off*. I'm as good as new. No lingering pain, no need to sneak off and see physiotherapists on the sly so no one would find out.

And a great thing about having no contact with Vance, only seeing him around the facilities every now and then, is all that pent-up, sexually frustrated energy I have toward him has gone into my recovery.

Boone, the team doc, and Coach have all cleared me to go back to playing. In practice, I've been killing it.

I'm as quick as before, strong, and Asher and I have been on the same wavelength. I keep up with him, and it's all back to normal. But right now, out here in a real game, where the hits are harder, I'm slower than a turtle in mud.

I'm hesitant.

And North Carolina is kicking our asses.

No matter what I do, I can't find the fucking puck, and when I do, I lose it almost immediately because I pass too soon or let North Carolina's defensemen strip it from me in fear of getting hit.

This is a fucking disaster.

Coach pulls me, and I don't fucking blame him. Our line gets the least amount of ice time we have all season, and I know it's because of me.

We manage to pull off a win, thanks to the rest of the team, but while everyone else celebrates, I stalk down the chute with my head down because that was fucking embarrassing.

You know it's bad when even Asher is trying to make me feel better.

"It was your first game back. No big deal."

Only, it is a big deal. A huge fucking deal.

And then the worst that could happen does. Because of course.

The locker room is opened to reporters wanting to get sound bites and quick interviews, and Langford Trest heads straight for me.

Asher turns, practically blocking me from the camera and from Langford, but it's no use.

"As much as I love hearing 'Eat shit and die' from you when I ask how you think your brother feels about your performance, Dalton, I was hoping to get a few questions in with Quinn seeing as he's freshly healed and back on the ice."

Freshly healed, yes, but could tonight's disaster performance really count as being back on the ice? I don't think so.

But unlike Asher, I don't have the balls to swear at reporters, so I turn to face the music with a strained smile on my face and an out-of-control heart rate.

"Slow start back," Langford says.

"I'm thankful we have such a great team to ease me back into the game."

"How's the injury? Were you in pain out there?"

Yeah, internal pain about how crappy I was playing. "I'm all healed. It's just a matter of getting into the groove."

"You're one of the lowest-scoring forwards for the season—"

Now I'm gritting my teeth. "Yeah, that happens when you need to have half the season off. Rest assured, I'm going to make up for lost time. Now, if you'll excuse me, I need to go make sure I cool down properly so I don't reinjure myself."

And while I'm at it, I might go ahead and cry.

That pressure—that weight sitting on my chest—telling me I need to push through and perform claws at me again. It weighs me down, threatening to pull me under, but I can't let it.

I can't push past my limits, or my whole life could crumble.

I just have to get my edge back.

I had it once; I can do it again.

From here on out, nothing but perfect games.

CHAPTER FOURTEEN

VANCE

The rhythmic thud and whir of a treadmill gives me the heads-up someone's already here. The facilities have been open for half an hour, but as I step into the room, there's Quinn, drenched in sweat and running like his life depends on it.

And considering he's a hockey player fresh off a shitty game, he probably thinks it does.

He hasn't seen me, and I could easily sneak away, but standing here, seeing him in the flesh again ... I *miss* him. The flirting and blushing and stammering. The crackle of *something* in the air between us. And I sort of just want to talk to him again.

The distance has done nothing for me, so is there a point in continuing to act like strangers around each other?

Probably, but I'm not gonna.

I dump my bag onto the floor and cross the room, trying not to startle him, but he's in the zone.

"Don't do this," I say when I'm close enough.

Quinn startles but thankfully doesn't go ass over. "Do what?"

"Punish yourself."

"M'not."

"Turn off the machine."

He huffs but hits the button to slow the belt, and I wait him out until he jogs to a stop. His chest is moving rapidly, T-shirt drenched around the neck, hair a sweaty mess, and I'm not proud of the dirty, dirty places my mind goes.

I swallow and drag my gaze away. "I saw the game last night."

"Ah. So you're talking to me again because of the pity?"

"Or because I saw you in here running your ass off and wanted to make sure you weren't about to reinjure yourself."

He chuckles. "Relax, Commando. Boone's given me the all clear. I'm one hundred percent."

"Didn't look that way last night."

"Ouch. You're really trying to make me relive it, aren't you?" Quinn grabs his towel and wipes over his face and neck before moving to the mats.

"Why were you hesitating last night?"

"I wasn't. Just came off an injury, remember?"

"Yeah, but if you're one hundred percent, that doesn't explain the early passes. The left-side stops. All that time you spent on the bench."

He groans and flops backward, arms splayed out to the side and T-shirt pulled up and showing off his abs. The blond hairs there catch the light, and this is exactly why I'm supposed to be staying away from him. I hate that I *want* to give in.

"Why are you pointing out how terrible I was? Did the last few weeks make you forget how delicate hockey players are?"

I laugh and sit down opposite him. "Leg out."

He peeks up at me from his place on the ground. "What are you doing?"

"Stretching with you."

Quinn immediately pushes back up to sitting. "You're not going to run off?"

I shrug but don't answer him, just wait for him to take the same position as me.

"No answer? Seriously? I've been so good at staying away from you and not pushing, and now here you are, willingly being around me. Did you … umm, did you get over me that quickly?"

"Stop talking," I beg.

"First you complained that I only made noises, and now you're complaining that I'm talking too much. I can't win with you."

He's right about that. Nothing he does will ever be right because *everything* he does is sexy as hell, and I wish I could stop looking at him that way. "I …" *Lie, lie, lie.* "I don't see any reason why we should avoid each other here. Other people are around. The next away game, I'll be the only trainer, and it's childish to keep this distance between us. Someone's bound to pick up on it eventually." I don't mention that O'Hennessy has already asked me about it.

"So I can come to you for massages again?" he asks, cheeky expression on his face.

"Why don't we worry about that if it happens?"

The innocent smile he gives me sets me very, very on guard. I don't even bother calling him on it because while I know that Quinn pushing would be the *worst* thing, I want him to anyway.

"Now, what happened in the game?"

His lightness completely disappears again. "Urgh, it was terrible."

"Yep."

"I couldn't get out of my head. Every single hit I took, I was like, *is this it*, and I knew I was being ridiculous, but I couldn't switch it off."

"Come on. Stretch while we talk." We get into mirrored positions, on one knee with the other leg stretched out to the side. "I don't think it's an uncommon fear."

"What do you mean?"

"Hockey's one of the things that make you *you*. And your career is something you've had to fight hard for. You're an amazing player, but I've noticed—even before you got injured—that you get in your own way some-times."

"Ah, so I've been shit for a while, then?"

"Did I say that?"

"In your super-professional way, you did."

I shake my head at his ridiculousness. "Or maybe the injury isn't the only thing that's got you in your head.

Maybe you got injured *because* of whatever's going on up here." I tap my temple.

His cute face drops into contemplation as we go through the rest of the stretches. I help out with correcting some of his form, not daring to actually touch him like I would if he was any other player.

It's nice. Just working beside each other in silence.

"This is basically our first date," he says out of nowhere.

I burst out with laughter. "I think I liked it better when you couldn't talk to me."

"Don't get me wrong, you still make my brain go dumb sometimes, but it helps knowing you do—*did*?—like me."

Knowing that he's very unsubtly asking if there's still something there, I skip over it. "How do I make your brain go dumb?"

"A lot of the time, it happens just being around you."

"It's not dumb right now."

"But mostly, it's whenever you say anything even remotely sexual."

Ooh, I'm gonna have fun with that. "I have no idea what you mean."

"You know, like …" He tries to think of something.

"Better get there quicker. It's going to be hard in the office today since I'm doing it solo."

He covers his face with one large hand. "Like *that*."

"What? I just meant things are going to be *tight* for me today."

Quinn shoves me gently, and even though he lets go right away, the place he touched *burns* through my long-sleeved shirt. "This is to get me back for the day I was with Boone, isn't it?"

"Which one?" I swear, over the last few weeks, even though I tried to avoid him, this place isn't as big as it seems. And every time we'd cross paths while Quinn was on the bed, he'd make the most ridiculously suggestive remarks. *Stiff, my ass.* I can just tell Boone is all but resigned to something happening between us.

Which pissed me off at first. My cock isn't a jack-in-the-box. I can keep it contained. Only now I'm seeing Quinn again, now it's just us, talking and joking around, I'm not so sure that's true. He's got this edge of innocence inside a big, muscled man that really does it for me. The baby face, the stache, the gold eyes hesitantly meeting mine from under his thick lashes.

I grunt as my cock thickens, and these athletic pants don't leave a lot to the imagination. Trying to be as subtle as I can manage, I shift around and draw my knees up in front of me. Unlucky for me though, Quinn clocks the movement, and realization lights up his eyes.

He checks the door and leans in. "Are you hard right now?"

"Inappropriate."

"More inappropriate than getting a boner over one of your players?" He's way too happy about this.

"Hey, I saw your hockey stick every time I worked on you, so you sure as hell can give me this one free pass."

"Sure I could." His grin is beautiful. "I just don't wanna."

"So back to this head stuff ..." I say, trying to steer the conversation back to safer grounds like his issues. But I know immediately that I've said the wrong thing when the amusement slides from his face and his tongue darts out over his bottom lip.

I point at him. "No."

"Didn't say anything."

"Tell that to your face."

"Maybe I'm the one who needs distance from you? How am I supposed to skate all day, thinking of this?"

"Probably better than you skated last night, thinking about whatever you were thinking about."

He narrows a glare at me. "Not gonna move on from that, are you?"

"Nope. So spill. Why are you so afraid of being sent back to the AHL? It's still professional hockey. You still get to play. Sure, it's not the big leagues, but it's a far cry from an office job."

"I don't really know. Obviously, disappointment and failure come into it, but I think it's more than a normal amount, you know?"

"I'd say so, considering you were willing to risk your body to stay in the game."

Quinn adjusts his position and sits flat on the mats. "I already told you coming out didn't go well for me. But not just the boyfriend thing; it also got into my head. The need that I have to be better than everyone to still be a valid player. It was like that with my dad too. It's why I first got into sports. I knew that I was different, and I wanted to prove to him I was still worthy of being his son. Which I know is super fucking messed up, and he never put that pressure on me—even when I came out to him, it went fine. But hearing the way some of the other parents talked about kids on my little league team, and football, and all the other sports I played until I landed on hockey when I was like … ten?"

"That's a lot for a kid to take on."

"Yeah …"

I shift closer because I want to hug him but can't. I'm just hoping the proximity helps. "Have you ever thought to talk to someone about it?"

"Like a shrink?"

"Yep."

"Fuck no." He laughs. "It's not like I've had some major trauma or anything—"

"That doesn't exclude you from having issues you need to work through. I'm not going to tell you what to do, but while hockey has so many great things about it— the family unit, the health benefits from exercise, travel, meeting people, working on good causes—and yeah, the money too—there's also a massive downside."

"Which is?"

"This stereotype of the *crazy* hockey player. The guy who has a tooth knocked out, spits it on the ice, and goes on to score a hat trick. The guy who goes gloves off for every little hit. Those players with penalty box stats and the almost hero worship some of them get for losing their shit each game. *Those* guys don't see a doctor. *Those* guys don't need to worry about mental health. They're *manly men*." I lift an eyebrow his way. "Sound familiar?"

Quinn's face turns sheepish. "I get what you're saying—trust me, between Ezra and Oskar, I know my fair share of dudes who probably need a head check."

"And it's not a bad thing."

"No, I know. But I'm not in that deep. I'm just playing head games with myself. I just have to get out of that mindset."

I want to push and tell him to talk to someone—even one or two sessions could help—but I said I wouldn't tell him what to do, and I won't. I've given him my thoughts, and he's a grown-ass man who can make his own choices. It sucks because I believe in taking care of your mind as much as your body, but like I couldn't stop him from getting that tear, I can't stop him from pushing through with this.

What I can do is what I didn't with his leg. I'm going to help him before it gets worse this time.

"We're going to work on it," I say.

"What?"

"I'm going to help you with your head."

Quinn groans. "There you go with the dirty talk again."

I laugh just as I hear voices coming down the hall. That's my cue to get moving. "Who would have thought Dick Dick Quinn has a filthy mind?"

"Oh, trust me. Fantasy You knows."

Is he … does he mean …

"Look at that. I've made *you* speechless for once."

I turn and walk away. "Why do I get the feeling I'm going to be telling you to behave a lot in the future."

"Because you're a very smart man."

CHAPTER FIFTEEN

QUINN

My game doesn't turn around. Not even a little. The team is skating by—pun intended—on small wins, and while they're on a hot streak, I'm in the biggest scoring dry spell of my life. That goes for off the ice as well because Vance and I are still dancing around each other and keeping to his rules of only interacting when others are around so we're not tempted to paw at each other's clothes and go to pound town.

It's getting to a point where I'd totally be okay with having sex with him in front of the team just to get out some of this frustration.

Sexual frustration, professional frustration, and every other kind of frustration. There's nothing more infuriating than watching your teammates' sloppy play, knowing you can do better, but then when it's your turn on the ice, you fucking choke.

I'm not surprised that Coach has shuffled the lines since I've been back, and I'm put on fourth line while rookie Ducre fills in for me on third alongside Asher like he did while I was out injured. We're winning, so Coach is reluctant to throw me back where I was. It could break the streak.

But if I'm honest, it's going to break soon anyway because we're getting by on pure luck at this point. Some hockey god has to be staring down at us from heaven and rooting for us.

Fuck knows we're not getting by on talent.

I grunt as we leave the ice in New York, taking out another win by a single point that Asher managed to get in at the last second so we didn't have to go into overtime.

Me, on the other hand, I haven't scored since I've been back. Not once. Not even one measly little goal.

We head down the chute, and I'm starting to get déjà vu. The team is celebrating, but I can't bring myself to match them. I used to believe a W is a W no matter how you get it, but when it feels like I haven't contributed to it, it's like I don't deserve it.

I glance toward the open door of Vance's borrowed office in Madison Square Garden, and even though my leg and groin are good, the first chance he's free, I'm going to ask him to help me stretch it out. Maybe his hands on me will calm the growing pressure.

He said he was going to help me with my head, but he's yet to get through to me.

No matter what he tries—telling me to skate for fun to get out of my head, linking me to countless articles on my career and how nearly every sportscaster has at one point said I'm the next big thing in hockey—every attempt has only managed to put more pressure on me as a player. To step up my game.

What if my time off killed my mojo permanently?

I cool down with a defeated air around me that must be so pungent no one wants to come near me, but it's probably better that way, and when I notice Asher slip out of Vance's office with some ice on his swollen jaw from a punch he took in a fight tonight, I make my way into the treatment room.

"What can I help you with?"

I jump up on the bed. "There's this annoying ache in my groin. Make it feel better?"

"You're such a shit," he mutters.

"It's mean to call your client that. Especially one that's hurrrting."

Vance appears above me, his face no longer holding that hint of amusement. "Did you really hurt yourself?"

"Not my groin. Just my pride. Though, I wouldn't mind stretching out my adductor. I've been a bit slack on doing that lately, and a smart man once told me I had to keep it up if I wanted to retain its strength."

"That doesn't sound like something I would say," he deadpans.

"Oh, you didn't. It was Boone."

Vance barks out a laugh. "Okay, I'll help you stretch, but you need to be good."

"I'll be a good boy," I purr. "I promise."

He glares at me.

"Okay, starting now. I swear."

Yet, the second his hands are on me, giving my tired muscles an amazing massage, my cock doesn't adhere to the rules. Vance's fingers work into my most sensitive places, and it takes all I have not to moan.

"Quinn …" Vance warns.

"It's a natural bodily reaction. I can't help it. Those were your words."

Vance closes his eyes. "I can't afford to get fired. I can't afford to get fired."

I love seeing this side of Vance, but it does make me think. "Can I ask you something?"

"If it's why we're not sleeping together yet, I'm going to go with no. You can't ask me."

"It's not exactly that, but I'm curious. Before, you know, when our roles weren't doing this Freaky Friday thing where you're the bumbling idiot, and I somehow have game—"

"What is your point?"

"When did it change for you?"

Vance's hand freezes on my upper thigh, and at this point, it probably looks like he just has his hand up my shorts.

So much for being professional.

"I'm not sure change is the right word." He pulls his hands away from me and brings over a stool to sit at the bedside. "I've always found you to be an attractive guy, but I always thought your body's reaction to me happened with Boone and O'Hennessy too. I was under the impression your dick was just very happily living its best life."

I laugh.

"But then ... then I overheard you say you had to get over your crush on me, and everything suddenly made sense." Vance looks away and lowers his voice. "My attraction to you was manageable up until then because I knew you were off-limits. I tried to explain away my reasons for following you and Dalton to that bar, but they were thin at best."

I'm torn on whether I'm supposed to feel good about that or not. Like, yeah, I'm super happy he feels even a smidge of the attraction I do for him, but only wanting to act on it after it's pointed out that I'm into him kinda makes it seem like a consolation prize.

Vance taps my shoulder. "You're not supposed to be thinking about this. Maybe this is why you're struggling out there on the ice."

"Noticed it's not improving, huh?"

"No offense, but you're not exactly hiding it well."

"I don't know how to fix me."

"First of all, we don't have to fix you. We have to fix that little voice inside your brain telling you to hold back."

"Well, I'm all out of ideas."

Vance grins. "I'm not. Don't go out with the team tonight. I'll swing by your room and pick you up."

"Ooh, are we finally going on a date?"

"Nope. Though, we are going to get sweaty."

"In thirty-degree weather?"

"Yup."

I have no idea what he has planned, but I'm interested.

All of my interest evaporates when he knocks on my door and the first thing he says is "Grab your running shoes."

"Decline."

He's in sweats and a beanie that covers his warm brown hair and looks ready for a workout. "You want out of your head or not? We're going running."

"In Manhattan? In the middle of the night? Oh, I get it, you're trying to get me killed. Or to have the threat of being killed so I will change my perspective on hockey. It's just a game. It's not life or death. For me, it is. Hockey is my life. I've sacrificed a lot to get here. I'm still sacrificing things for it." I wave my hand over his body.

"Stop being so dramatic. We're just going to go for a run."

I don't understand how that's going to get me out of my head, but I relent. "Fine. But if I get stabbed, I get to hold it over your head forever."

"Forever might be short if you bleed to death."

"Okay, now I'm worried you're the one who's going to do the stabbing."

Vance sighs. "Stop whining, and get your shoes on. And maybe add some layers."

I do it, and then we head outside. It's not snowing, but it's cold enough to.

I refuse to get started. "I don't see how going for a run will get me out of my head. Do you know how much running I've done since my injury? It was like it was the only thing you and Boone would let me do to prove how strong it is."

"Eh, the run is just to tire your brain. It's where we're running to that I wanted to show you."

"Unless we're running toward what's inside your pants, I don't think I'm interested."

"How can you still be going on about sex when your career is on the line?"

"It's all I have in my life right now. Why won't you let me have it?"

Vance cocks his head. "Sex or talking about it?"

I throw up my hands. "Either."

"Why aren't you having sex? Other than your injured leg. You could have any guy you want."

I stare pointedly at him.

"You could have any guy you want who is queer and you don't work with. How about that?"

He's waiting for an answer—a proper one—but I don't want to tell him I've been too focused on my career. I don't want to point out that the one and only time I was interested in hooking up, I tore my groin and he was there to rescue me.

"I'm not waiting around for you if that's what you're asking." We've been standing outside for a few minutes now, and my words come out with puffs of visible air with my breath.

Vance laughs. "It's not, but now I'm questioning if that's the case."

"Oh, look at that. Time to run." I take off at a jog, but his voice follows after me.

"Wrong way!"

I turn back around and jog after him now, letting him lead the way.

It has to only be about ten blocks or so, but I have no idea where he's taking me until we come to a quiet area overlooking some bridge. It's not the Brooklyn Bridge but one of the other ones. I forget all their names. It's the one that goes over Roosevelt Island with the cable cars.

"You brought me to … the Hudson River? To … drown me?"

"Stop with the killing jokes. And that's not the Hudson. It's the East."

"Fine. You brought me to a bridge to, what? Tell me to build one and get over it?"

Vance breaks into laughter. "No, but that's actually a good motto." He goes to look out over the railing, at the water below us, the bridge lights in front of us, and the picturesque city behind us.

"I have a thing with bridges. Especially ones in Manhattan."

"You like … bridges."

"Yup. Did you ever do that team-building exercise where you were split into groups and you had to build a bridge out of Popsicle sticks, and the one that could withstand the most weight won?"

I pass a confused look over him. "Maybe in high school? I can't remember."

"It has structure, and some bridges have amazing architecture. It's not a big thing, and it's not like I go around

133

collecting models of bridges or anything, but it's just something about me that's solely about having an interest outside of work. Maybe you need to find an interest outside of hockey. Something else to focus on for a while until you get your game back. You've put so much pressure on yourself, on the team, on your career, that I don't think you've done anything but lived and breathed hockey for the last six years."

I swallow hard because he'd be right about that.

"You need to find something that's just for you. Even if it's staring at a stupid bridge in the middle of the night with your team trainer who you like to tease."

I'd like to do a hell of a lot more than tease him. "I know of something else I'm interested in." I step toward him.

At first, he doesn't understand what I'm implying, and my nerves tell me to back the hell off, but my body won't let me.

I know this isn't what he had in mind when he brought me here. He's trying to help my game. But the thing is, while he makes a point, there's only one thing I've been obsessive about since hockey.

"What's that?" he asks, his voice a rasp as I close the distance between us.

Without letting myself chicken out, I press against him, put my hand on his hip, and whisper, "You."

CHAPTER SIXTEEN

VANCE

Quinn's proximity steals the night from around me until all that's left is his scent, his vulnerable eyes shining in the light from the bridge, and the absence of those little puffs of breath. He's frozen. Waiting. Probably second-guessing this spark of confidence, and goddamn, my heart is racing.

I knew I was smart to avoid touching him all this time because now his hand is on my hip, palm heavy through my layers, us almost chest to chest, the chaos of *no*s inside my head just … switches off. A long, stuttered breath leaves him, and I'm sucking down enough oxygen for us both. Seeing him so unsure, so—fuck, I don't wanna say tortured, but that's how I feel—is what does it.

I'm done holding back.

I step forward, bringing our chests together as I wrap a hand around the back of his neck, and then he's meeting me halfway. Our mouths crash together, and the second we make contact is the greatest thrill of my life. The want inside me bursts from the cage I had it trapped in and floods my body, filling me with an uncontrollable urge to move closer, take more.

My lips part, and Quinn immediately follows, tongue surging forward and stroking mine. His nose and cheeks are cold, but his mouth is blazing hot, and I wish he wasn't wearing the stupid beanie so I could twist my fingers through that golden hair that drives me wild. I bet it would be all sweaty and messy, perfect to tug on.

Quinn grunts into my mouth, fists gripping the back of my jacket like he never wants me to let him go. Joke's on him, though, because I'm hooked. His body, his kiss, the perfect scratch of his facial hair.

I'd brought him out here for perspective, and look at me getting a hit of my own.

We're both consenting adults; we both really fucking tried to stay away, and this is where we ended up anyway. The kiss is burning up the cool night air, bringing a smile to my face and making me feel like I could fucking fly.

"Urgh, Vance," Quinn murmurs, rocking his hard cock against my hip. "Need you. Want you so bad."

His desperate words break the haze enough to remind me the rest of the world exists. The water rushing past below, the lights of the city, the few cars zipping past. I'm panting and painfully hard, tempted to say fuck it and grind up against him anyway. But ending the night on a misdemeanor will not support my case with Boone that I can do this and remain professional.

"I know." I kiss my way along his jaw, not wanting to break this bubble of lust we've fallen into. "But not here."

"So where? The team is at the hotel ..."

"Could get a room somewhere else."

He presses his shiny lips together. "And be seen? I … I don't want to get you in trouble. Or be traded."

"Same page." My mind is in overdrive as I run my nose up his cheek. There has to be *somewhere*. But I have no car, an alleyway in Manhattan doesn't guarantee privacy, and him coming to my room could be seen by anyone considering I'm on the same floor as the team. "Shit."

"Why can't we be in Buffalo?" he whines. "I have a whole house we could cover in cum."

"Now, that's a picture."

Quinn's forehead drops onto my shoulder. "There's nowhere, is there?"

"You'd think in a city this size it wouldn't be so hard."

"Don't say *hard*."

That almost makes me laugh, but I'm way too sexually frustrated. If we can't find a place to get off together, I will one hundred percent be going back to my room to jerk off over him, and I haven't even had a chance to see his body. I want fap material, damn it.

"Wait …"

"Yeah?" His head snaps up off my shoulder.

"Don't get too excited. It's not what we want, but it's something."

"What is it?"

"You share with Dalton, right?"

"Right."

"Think he'll be asleep?"

Quinn frowns. "We can't in my room. I—"

I push forward with my idea. "I was thinking ... well, since we can't make it work, we'll both be going back to jerk off, right?"

His lips pinch. "I guess."

"So we'll do it together. Video call me from your bathroom."

Quinn's eyes light up. "That'll do." He grabs my hand and all but drags me back the way we came.

"What if Dalton's awake though?"

"Then he's going to hear some things he doesn't want to hear, so he better hope he's sleeping."

Good enough for me. We jog back to the hotel, pushing harder than we did on the way out, and while my cock calms down enough to let me run, I'm at half-mast the whole way there. Getting to see Quinn completely naked? Fuck. I'm going to be ruined after this. I take a second to check how much I care, and uhhh ... I care zero amounts.

Just before we reach the bright lights spilling from our hotel doors, Quinn tugs me to a stop. He glances around as he steps close, and his hand grazes my bulge.

"Ooomph."

I laugh. "You good now?"

"One more thing. This can't be it. When we get back to Buffalo, I need to touch you. Promise me."

"Easiest deal I've ever made."

His grin lights me up inside. "Race you."

We both hurry across the lobby, trying not to draw suspicion, and ride the elevator up together, but the second the doors open to our floor, I take off. We're at opposite ends of the hall, and I hear his door open just as I get my key card out. It takes me two tries to get my door open, and as soon as I slam it behind me, I'm kicking off my sneakers and stripping out of my clothes. I leave a long trail behind me on the way to the bed. I grab my lube, switch on the lamp, and when I go to pull up Quinn's number, his name flashes on my screen.

I smirk and swipe to answer. "Smartass—"

His long, naked body fills the screen, and my words dry up. He's standing in the bathroom, phone propped up somewhere so he's completely in frame, and I greedily drink in the image.

"Damn, Quinnie ..." I shift my legs further apart as my dick plumps. His is already full, head red and shiny, with a slight, beautiful curve to the shaft. "I hate this idea."

His chuckle is as husky as my voice. "I'll hate it less when I can see you."

"Good point." I grab one of the billion pillows piled on the bed and set it at my feet. Then I prop my phone up and open my legs nice and wide.

"Aw, shit." His hand closes around his cock and gives it a tight squeeze. "Damn, that's an angle."

My gut warms as I wrap my hand around my cock as well, a hum slipping out at the friction. I'm blindingly frustrated that I can't kiss him, but I'm going to the second we're back in Buffalo, and that's going to have to be good enough for now.

I check my camera and prop myself up, making sure my balls, dick, and abs are all in the shot.

"Want your face too," he rasps, stroking himself.

"Bossy." I add another pillow until I have the angle right.

He confirms it when he groans. "Right there."

"You can talk."

He smiles, the bashful one that makes him flush all over. "You've seen my dick before."

"Not properly." I'm greedily staring now though. "I was professional. I didn't let myself look."

"You have way more self-control than me."

"I've noticed." I crack my lube and pour a generous amount over my cock. My hand follows it down my shaft, and the smooth slide has me moaning. I'm oversensitive, burning hot, ready to show Quinn how I come. Knowing he's watching me touch myself, and knowing he probably feels the exact same way as me, sends a thrill to my balls.

"You are so unbelievably hot," he mutters, hand stroking long, hard pulls over his length. "I don't know where to look."

"Ngh. When you're with me, I'm going to have that same issue. Do I kiss you? Lick your neck? Bite your nipples? Or suck on that glorious fucking cock of yours?"

He lets out a breathy laugh. "All of it. I can't wait to taste you. To feel your cock on my tongue." His voice hitches, and he lifts his hand to his mouth. I watch him stroke his precum-covered fingers over his tongue as his eyes go glassy. "It's like I can taste you already."

"Don't stop touching yourself." I'm already dangerously close to the edge, and I don't want to let go before he does.

Quinn's big hand immediately wraps back around his cock. His grunts and the slick sounds of him beating off are loud, and I can only imagine if Dalton is there that he can probably hear everything. Every hoarse sound from Quinn and every filthy word from me.

But I'm so fucking past caring that I don't let it stop me.

"Play with your balls."

He does, free hand tugging on them and rolling them in his palm. His lips are parted, and I can just picture sliding my cock between them, stroking the head over his tongue, watching as those heavily lidded eyes fill with tears as I fuck that pretty mouth.

I was right in thinking his hair would be a mess from his beanie; it looks like it will after I've gripped it in my fingers. Run my hands through it while I grind against him. The feel of that gorgeous, curved shaft sliding against mine, covering me in his precum, throbbing against my desperate skin as he shoots.

Will he be quiet or loud? Shudder or stock-still?

These aren't things I should ever know about a player, but I'm in deep now. No turning back, even if I wanted to.

Quinn's abs contract, and his bicep flexes with every stroke. His expression is the most checked out I've ever seen it, and I'm already addicted to the view. Wanting to see it again and again. Wishing I could make out exactly how dark those golden eyes have gone.

His head drops back, exposing the thick column of his throat and his jutting Adam's apple.

I want to reach through the phone and drag my tongue over him, grip his hips and swallow his length down. Feel the smooth round head of his cock breach my throat as his thighs shudder under my hands.

I want his head thrown back like that when I'm fucking him. Or he's fucking me. My thighs twitch as my balls tighten with that thought. My skin feels too restrictive. Pricked with sweat. Ready to burst.

I bring my finger to my mouth to get it nice and wet, then slide it behind my balls. Quinn's breath hitches on a gasp as I press my finger into my hole and search around for—

Bingo.

Pleasure sweeps through me.

"Come, Quinn. Please come."

But when I glance back at the screen, he's beat me to it. One leg is tensed, free hand gripping the sink as he strokes himself through his orgasm. The lines of cum dripping down his abs is the most erotic thing I've ever seen, and I finally let go.

The tingles from my ass increase the building ache in my balls, then the pressure releases. My toes grip the sheets as my hips lift from the bed, cock seeking to prolong every last wave of pleasure. I twitch through what feels like a never-ending orgasm, but once it's over, the high ends too fast.

I sag onto the bed, catching my breath, itchy with the knowledge that he's a whole hallway away. Close enough that I could have him in my arms within minutes, but with way too many obstacles in our way to actually do it.

"Are you ... was that okay?" he asks, and when I glance back at my phone, it's just his face on the screen.

I wipe off my hands on the sheets and pick my phone up as well. I hate that he can sound so insecure after something so incredible. "Stop it."

"Stop what?"

"Thinking I'm going to regret it." I smile. "That was fucking amazing. And I'm glad it happened."

His eyes light up. "Yeah?"

Oh, fuck, I want to kiss him. "Next time we're together, I'll show you just how much."

CHAPTER SEVENTEEN

QUINN

I slump against the vanity in the bathroom, staring at my phone and wondering if that phone call really happened.

Or the kiss by the not-Brooklyn Bridge.

Or anything at all between Vance and me.

I'm sated but in disbelief, like the blank screen in front of me might have been that way the whole time, and I imagined Vance's desperation, his resolve cracking.

My only regret is not taking the risk and going into his room, but if we'd been caught, we would've had to explain what we were doing, and considering I still can't believe anything happened between us at all, that's an answer we don't have.

Or, at least, I don't.

Vance had a lot of opportunities to stop. He didn't have to accept my call or go through with anything. But he did. And he said next time. Like it's definitely going to happen again when we get back, but you know, in the same room as each other.

It's something to look forward to while simultaneously dreading the rest of this road trip, but at the same time,

I'm not going to get my hopes up. There's another week before we're home, which will give Vance plenty of time to change his mind and go back to saying it's too unprofessional for us to be together.

I would understand, but I'll also be crushed by disappointment.

I don't get interested in guys like this. Don't obsessively lust over them.

I'm nervous we just fucked everything up while wanting nothing more than to kiss him again. Hold him. Next time, have our naked skin pressed against each other instead of via video call.

There's nothing better than passing out after a good orgasm, but now that we've crossed that line, I'm too wired to even try. So instead, I pull up my boxer briefs, shuck off my sweats from around my ankles, and climb into bed with my phone on dark mode and brightness turned right down so I don't disturb Asher.

And then I think about what Vance said. About his weird interest in bridges—a completely random fact about him that has nothing to do with his job. No matter how much I search my brain for things I'm interested in, things I like to do outside of hockey, I can't find anything. Because everything, in a roundabout way, relates back to hockey.

Going to the gym: to stay fit so I can play hockey.

Cooking: to eat the right foods to stay on top of my game. I like experimenting with low-calorie, high-protein foods for muscle growth to make it, you know, palatable.

But again, it has to do with hockey. Otherwise, I'd make myself unhealthy fried food that's delicious but makes me sluggish on the ice.

I follow weird team superstitions because of the off chance it could affect our games. I don't actually believe in any of them.

Maybe I can jump on Vance's bridge obsession. I'm definitely more of a fan of not-Brooklyn Bridge after tonight than ever before. Hmm, maybe I should find out what bridge that actually was.

After a quick google, it tells me my new favorite spot on Earth is the Queensboro Bridge. Who would've thought something that leads to Queens could bring such joy?

I need advice and to talk to the Collective, so I shoot off a message to them all, setting up one of our infamous group chats for the morning before we leave to head for DC.

Eventually, I do get to sleep, only to be woken, what feels like seconds later, by Asher standing over me. He nudges me with his foot and murmurs something about me possibly being dead.

I squint up to find him talking to his phone screen. "Wha?"

"You're the one who arranged for this Queerdo meeting, and then you sleep in?" He turns his phone toward me, and there's a bunch of little boxes with everyone's faces.

"Nergh." I yawn and sit up, running a hand through my messy hair.

"You look like shit," Ezra says. "Who do we have to beat up?"

I laugh at his big brotherness. "No one. I just had a question."

"A question that couldn't be asked via text?" Asher scowls. "You're making me deal with these people before coffee o'clock? It's like you want me to hate you, Quinnie."

I go to ask my question—what their thing outside of hockey is—but instead, I blurt something I shouldn't. "I hooked up with the team's trainer last night."

Gasps echo through the speaker while Asher drops his phone completely.

"Vance threw you a bone?" Asher bends to pick his phone back up and then sits next to me on the bed. "Have you guys seen Vance? Super hot, super out of Quinn's league."

"Thanks," I mutter.

"Oh, looks-wise, you're on par, but he's so put together, and you ..."

Okay, fair. "I know. I'm a mess."

"You blush around him, for fuck's sake. You can't string a sentence together, and—"

"Well, I got over that. We went for a run last night because I'm too in my head, and that's why I'm sucking on the ice—"

"I bet he was sucking off the ice last night too," Oskar cuts in. Because of course he does.

"I'm not giving any of you the details. My point of this call isn't Vance. It's something he said."

"Do me harder?" Oskar asks.

"That's not where that goes?" Ezra says.

"I hate you all," I grumble. "My point, if the two slutbags will stop interrupting—"

Now everyone else interrupts with sniggers.

I ignore it. "—is he pointed out that I have no interests outside of hockey, and maybe I'm struggling on the ice because my injury is affecting my ability to execute anything, and if maybe I didn't have so much pressure on hockey, that I might realize hockey isn't everything. If I can do that, I'll be some well-rounded person or whatever. That's when I realized the only interest I have outside of hockey is him, and I'm pretty sure he can't be my distraction from reality."

They're all silent for a beat, but then Ezra asks, "Why not? Sex is an awesome distraction that has nothing to do with hockey."

"Agreed," Oskar says. "Adding an element of danger to it is awesome too."

"Danger as in setting yourself on fire while you do it?" Asher asks.

"Like public sex, duh." Oskar's obviously in bed, his head resting back on a pillow, and he quickly looks beside him. "But I don't do that anymore, obviously."

There's a chuckle that comes from Lane, which makes me think he's lying, and they probably get it on publicly. With Lane being the PR master that he is, it's probably in a controlled environment.

"As much as I'd be on board for that, I don't think putting that kind of pressure on Vance is a good way to make him fall in love with me. Being all 'You're the only thing I have in my life outside of hockey' is enough to send any man running for the hills."

"Ugh," Ezra grunts. "People who equate sex with love. I'm out. I have no advice. Anton, you're up."

"Lane, your turn." Oskar hands his phone over to a very tired-looking Lane. It's easy to forget the West Coast is a few hours behind. Oops. That's probably why Tripp and Dex have missed the call too.

Anton shakes his head. "Ignore those hos. What about volunteering somewhere? I find giving back to the community somehow makes my lavish lifestyle not so … wasted. No, that's not the right word. It takes away the guilt of having super-nice things when some people don't even have a roof over their heads. Ugh, that makes me sound like I have some sort of hero complex."

"I get what you're saying, and maybe I could look into that. Though, throwing money at something isn't quite what I'm looking for."

"Tripp and Dex volunteer coach with a local LGBTQ team," Lane says.

"That still has to do with hockey," I point out.

When their ideas dry up, I realize I need to figure this out on my own. Because even though they have some great suggestions, none of them fit me.

"I'll find something to distract me from hockey."

Ezra's voice sounds far away, but I still hear it. "Until you do, enjoy all the sex with the guy we're going to have to check out next time we play each other."

I look up to the hockey gods. "Please let Boone be working that day."

We all end the call, and I'm no closer to figuring out who I am outside of hockey.

CHAPTER EIGHTEEN

VANCE

An entire week on the road didn't sound so bad before we left home, but goddamn it, every day is moving at a snail's pace. I see Quinn on the plane, in the hotel, during training, and my eyes are glued to him when he's on the ice. He loosens up fractionally with each game, but he's still not at the level he used to be.

It's so frustrating being on the outside and not being able to fix it for him. His adductor? I've got it. His head? Not so much. While I wasn't lying when I said I had interests outside of the game, when it comes to work/life balance, I need to get way better at managing myself. The thing is, going home to an empty house every night isn't as relaxing as it used to be, and there are only so many times I can call Joe or one of my other friends.

My gaze strays to where Quinn's sitting on the bench, watching the ice and dying to get back out there. He's the first choice I've made in a really, really long time that hasn't tied into work, and by choosing to explore what's between us, I'm putting the only thing I have going for me on the line. Boone was understanding, but that's no guarantee management will be, and yet, I'm taking the risk. I don't even know where exactly I want this to lead, but the voice in my ear is telling me it's worth finding out.

Maybe we'll have sex—in the same room this time—and Quinn will decide that's all he needed from me. I hope he doesn't, but you never know, and considering how long he's been building this up, the last thing I want is for him to walk away disappointed.

Coach signals for Quinn to get his ass back out there and calls the third line back in. Dalton and Ducre hit the benches first, and I head straight over to check on Dalton from the stray stick he just caught to the face.

"Take off your helmet."

"I'm fine."

Hockey players. They're all the same.

"Now, Dalton."

His permanent scowl deepens, and he wrenches it off. His cheekbone has a shiner coming through, and it's already red with shades of purple. There's no blood though, and the swelling isn't bad enough to indicate anything's broken under there. I grab a cold compress.

"Keep this on there. I'll have a new one ready each time you come off."

He huffs and pulls his helmet back on, then does as I say. Which is a goddamn miracle because Asher Asshole Dalton is being *compliant*. Maybe the heavens are shining down on me after all.

"You coming out tonight?" he asks like he doesn't want to but can't stop himself.

"Tonight?"

"Chenkin's birthday. The whole team's going."

I'm very, very tempted, but I don't know if it would look strange for me to go and hang out with the team. It's not unheard of, but it's not something I do often. Knowing Quinn will be there though … how do I say no to that?

"Do it," Müller says from Dalton's other side. "You're always going back to your room alone instead of coming out with us. It'll be a fun time."

I'm about to agree when Dalton jumps to his feet. "Fuck yes, Quinn!"

Holy shit, he scored.

I groan as I realize I missed it.

Dalton pats me on the shoulder and shoves the cold compress into my hand. "You've gotta come out now. We're celebrating that too." Then he takes off onto the ice, and I watch Quinn come off again, realizing that Dalton *knows*.

Even though I said I didn't care if he heard us, that was an in-the-moment thing. With the clarity of my brain not being dosed in dopamine, I'm not sure how I feel about it. Quinn and I haven't established anything between us, and until I know what this thing is, there's no point talking to Boone or management or whatever to make it official. And while Dalton seems to have Quinn's back, I have no reason to think he'd keep our secrets. If he gets drunk tonight, will he let it slip? Will the team find out?

I shake that uncomfortable thought off as I head Quinn's way.

"Congratulations."

"Thanks." He looks thrilled. Relieved. Everything about him radiates happiness. "It felt good."

"I bet it did." I conveniently leave off that I actually didn't see it. I doubt he'd be too disappointed since I was literally doing my job, but I don't want to say anything that will bring down his happiness. I clear my throat and add, "I hear it's Chenkin's birthday."

His gaze snaps from the ice to me. "You're coming out with us?"

"According to Dalton and Müller, I am."

It's goddamn adorable the way he tries to hold back his excitement. "Right. Good. Cool. I'll see you then?"

I wink. "Ferfect."

His head falls back with a laugh. "I'm never living that down, am I?"

"Literally never."

I'm called away for a lip bleed, and then it's one thing after another, and I don't get a chance to talk to Quinn for the rest of the night. We're on day five of seven, and I haven't had a chance to get him alone since the night we spent together. The team has been out celebrating their wins or going to dinner, or we've had a late flight out. I would have been happy to go for a run—no euphemisms—but we haven't even managed that. It's getting to a point where I just want the freedom to talk to him without a thousand people listening in, and I can't even have that. Secret relationships aren't worth the hype. Getting off on being caught? Fuck that. I wanna get off

154

on being able to ask Quinn how his day was and not get some caged answer.

The team is killing it with these East Coast games because we finish up with another win, thanks to Quinn's goal. For the first time since his injury, he actually walks away from the game with a smile on his face.

Which puts one on mine too.

Like after every game, I patch up cuts, check over injuries, and argue with Dalton over how much attention he has to give his injury. Fun times. And just like every game, I look for an opportunity to get Quinn alone and come up empty. Which I know professionally is for the best, but I want to spend time with him.

The team heads straight out to the bar in their suits while I run back to the hotel to shower and change. I'm nervous as I arrive and walk in, hoping it's not going to be completely obvious that I'm here for Quinn and no one else. I like the team, I'm glad we won, but if it wasn't for Quinn, I wouldn't be standing here.

So I force a deep breath, shut myself up, and make my way toward the back of the bar, where the team is already deep in the drinks. They have tomorrow off before one more game and a flight home right after it, so this is their last chance to celebrate before everyone returns to their families.

I spot Quinn almost immediately, hair tamed for once, sitting between Dalton and Chenkin and smack-talking them over something, judging by the way Chenkin roars with laughter. It almost makes me want to back away and leave him to it, but I force my feet in their direction. They've grouped a whole lot of tables and stools together midway between the pool tables and the bar, and with the exception of a few puck bunnies and people in team jerseys, the rest of the patrons are giving them a wide berth.

"Vance, you made it!" Müller yells, lifting a drink my way. "We got you one."

"Thanks, man." I down a long gulp to avoid looking at Quinn, even as every cell in my body is swirling with nerves and awareness of his presence. "Coach didn't come?"

Müller shakes his head. "We invited everyone, but apparently, you're the only one cool enough to come out with us."

"Cool or stupid?"

He laughs. "Depends where the night goes, I guess."

"After here? Back to the hotel. I'm not having Coach tear me a new asshole because I let his players fuck themselves up on their night off."

"Maybe we shouldn't have invited you."

"Tomorrow, when you're not locked up somewhere, you can thank me."

We tap our glasses together, and then I finally let myself look Quinn's way. He's staring right at me, not doing a damn thing to be subtle, and I wish this was one of those times Dalton would point out how stupid he's being.

It feels good though.

That level of attention directed my way.

It makes me want to call Boone and be like, "I'm taking Quinn back to my room tonight, okay, thanks, bye," but that isn't the kind of conversation you have over the phone. My first step is with Quinn.

Then I can factor in everyone else.

Against all rational thoughts, I approach him at the same time as a man in a Buffalo jersey approaches Dalton.

"Hey, cutie."

Dalton gives him the chilliest look I can imagine. "There's nothing cute about me."

"True. On the ice, you're incredible."

"Not just on the ice." Dalton's jaw tightens. "My boyfriend tells me all the time."

The man chuckles and steps close enough he can rest his hand on Dalton's thigh. "You're funny."

"Actually, I'm an asshole. And if you don't get your hand off a taken man, you'll find out just how much."

The guy snatches his hand up and steps back. "Geez, chill out."

"Eat shit and die."

The man flips him off and walks away while the three of us watch him go. The audacity of some fuckers.

"You're gonna get in trouble if you don't stop saying that," Quinn warns like it isn't the first time.

Dalton shrugs. "But West taught me not to lie and I *really* want them to eat shit and die."

I'm not even going to touch that.

"This seat taken?" I ask, nodding toward Dalton.

He rolls his eyes but immediately stands and heads for the bar without so much as a hello.

"You know," I say to Quinn, "that guy tries *really* hard to make people not like him."

"He has a big heart," Quinn says. "He just hides it really, really, really well."

"No arguments from me."

I take Dalton's vacated spot, subtly shifting my stool that much closer to Quinn's. Our thighs press under the table, and he lets out a little "meep" at the contact.

I burst out with laughter. "What was that?"

"I … I wasn't …" He looks around, but Chenkin is talking to Ducre, and the guys across the table are talking about a pool game. "I didn't expect that, okay?" He reaches under the table and gives my thigh a squeeze, which does nothing to help my neediness at being so close.

It's just lucky for me that he lets go immediately.

And this is what I wanted. Time to talk to him. To be one-on-one and not have to be so overly cautious about what we say. His team is distracted and drinking, and while most of them insert themselves into our conversation at some point, they don't pay us too much attention, especially when their pool tournament gets underway.

"I'm glad you came out."

"Me too. I worried it might be a bit obvious though."

"What would be?"

"That all I've been able to think about this entire trip is getting you into my bed."

Quinn's eyes light up. "Yeah?"

"What do you mean 'yeah'?" I nudge him with my elbow. "We've gotta work on your confidence. I already told you it's on once we're home."

He snorts into his beer. "It's not my confidence that's the issue. It's the fact I've wanted this for so long it doesn't feel real. I'm just waiting for the doubt to kick in."

"You'll be waiting a while. I might have been hesitant to cross any lines, but that ship's sailed, and honestly, I think it was only a matter of time."

"C-can I ask you something?" Hesitant Quinn is back.

"Always."

"Are you … you said things changed for you when you heard what I said. It's not … I'm not one of those last-man-on-Earth scenarios, am I?"

It takes me a second to even work out what the hell he's saying. And when I do, I want to laugh. At him. Because him thinking I only want this because he's my only option is ridiculous. "My job is to desensitize myself. To view whoever's on my bed as a makeup of limbs and muscle. It's clinical. Professional. Because it needs to be. It's always been harder with you, but I put it down to you getting all flustered, and I thought it was kinda cute. Then I heard you talking with Dalton, and the rest just … unfolded, I guess. You're one of the hottest men I've ever met, but you're also incredibly sweet and kind, and I like how you let yourself be vulnerable. You're also a stubborn ass, but I think I kind of like it."

His cheeks are flaming red again, and I eye them, pride welling in my chest. "Okay, I accept that."

"Thought you might."

"Do you think, since the whole team is here, that we could maybe sneak to your room?"

All the temptation is enough to burst. God, I want that. To drag Quinn out of here so I can see him naked and up close this time.

"I hate myself, but let's not risk anything. It's two long, *long* days. But the second we land back in Buffalo"—I lean closer so my lips are by his ear—"I'm going to kidnap you for your two days off, and I won't be letting you loose until I'm done."

CHAPTER NINETEEN

QUINN

The flight home to Buffalo has never seemed so long, and we're only coming from North Carolina, not even out west somewhere far away.

It's like the pilot knows I have plans to be dicked out and is flying slower or something.

When we finally start our descent, my gaze finds the back of Vance's head, who's sitting near the front of the plane. I try to send him telepathic thoughts that I'm coming for him as soon as we land, but I don't think it works.

Before we get too low in the sky where the seat belt sign would come on, Coach gets out of his seat and stands in front of us all.

"We had an absolutely amazing week on the road, and I wanted to tell you all before we land and you scurry off to celebrate or go home to see your families that I'm proud of how well we're doing this season. Not just these few away games but as a whole. We're on track to make the playoffs for the first time in over a decade, and I think we're building something amazing here. This is the team that could take us all the way if we put our heads down and keep our eyes on the prize."

Müller lets out a "Whoop," and the rest of the team cheers.

"There's just a bit of housekeeping I want to get out of the way before you write yourselves off for two days. One, don't forget to do weight training. You don't have to use our facilities, so I'm trusting you all to get it done. Two, don't get arrested."

Everyone laughs, and Asher yells, "Can't make any promises, Coach."

"Don't even joke, Dalton. You're the third thing I need to address."

A round of "Oooh" fills the plane, but Asher doesn't look scared.

"You need to stop telling reporters and puck bunnies to eat shit and die."

The whole team erupts into laughter.

"Why?" Asher asks. "They deserve it!"

More laughing.

"If a reporter asks you a question you don't like, say 'no comment'. And if you can't handle some attention from fans, maybe we need to put you through some PR training."

"If reporters stopped comparing me to my big brother and puck bunnies left me alone when I've told them I'm taken, there wouldn't be a problem."

"Unfortunately, that might be too much to ask of society," Coach says with a defeated tone.

"Fine," Asher grumbles. "Can I tell them to fuck off? Is that better or worse?"

Even though the vibe has gone down a notch or two into serious territory, there are still a few snickers.

"Jesus H. Christ," Coach mutters. "PR training starts tomorrow."

Asher goes to open his mouth, and I'm assuming he's about to tell *Coach* to eat shit and die, but whatever he was going to say doesn't come out. Asher might be impulsive, but he's not dumb.

"And there go your days off," I say as Coach makes his way back to his seat.

"How will you survive without me?"

My gaze finds the back of Vance's head again. "I think I'll manage."

Asher sighs when he realizes who I'm looking at. "I miss Kole."

I reach over to him and pinch his cheek. "Aww, poor baby."

His green eyes are murderous, and he swats my hand away.

"When's the next visit?"

"Spring break."

I want to cry for him. I've barely survived the last week without being able to be with Vance again. To go months? Well, actually, that wouldn't be much different to the last year that I've been lusting over the guy. Only now, I know what he tastes like. I know how firm his mouth is. How dominating his tongue can be.

Fuck, when are we going to land?

As soon as the damn wheels hit the tarmac, I practically jump out of my seat.

"Where's the fire?" Müller asks.

In my pants. Nope. Not saying that. "I'm just ready to get home." And naked. And filled.

Even though I rush, Vance doesn't have the same urgency, which means I'm waiting for him anyway.

He finally deplanes and catches up, an easy smile on his face while I'm sure I look like an impatient puppy waiting for its ball to be thrown, only I'm waiting for Vance's balls to be thrown in my mouth.

"Come to my place," he says, his voice low.

"I'll race you there. Just give me the address."

He chuckles. "Go home and shower and then head over. I have things I need to do first."

I eye him. "Is it the same thing I'll be doing in the shower? Yes is the only acceptable answer to get me to go home first."

"It might be. You'll just have to wait and see."

"You're a tease."

He steps back, and I almost follow him, wanting to be close to him, but then Coach waltzes past us, and I realize why.

Vance turns on his heel and says over his shoulder, "I'll text you the address."

—

I've never showered and got started on the prep part of sex faster in my life. I haven't bottomed for a long time, and even when I was with my ex, I didn't do it often, but fuck, if I get the chance tonight, I'm taking it.

And if Vance really was going home to prepare for me as well, then I'll take that too.

I'm like a starved man going to an all-you-can-eat buffet.

I hope Vance is fast at showering, or maybe I don't. I wouldn't mind walking in and watching him. Or joining. What's a little breaking and entering when it comes to sex? Wait, no, that sounds wrong.

Which means I force myself to drive the speed limit all the way to Vance's place, which turns out to be a town house close to the arena.

There's an entire row of connected houses, so I find the right one and park my car in his short drive.

Buffalo is considerably cheap compared to a lot of cities in the country, so Vance's place is on the nicer side but still modest.

It's newer than mine, which isn't hard to do, seeing as mine's like a hundred years old, but his home is probably still thirty years old. It's all brick, with a garage underneath and outside steps leading to his front door.

I tell myself to calmly walk up and knock. No running allowed. But when I reach the door, he swings it open before I even get the chance to raise my hand.

He immediately smiles, grips my jacket, and pulls me inside and against his body. His lips slam down on mine, and I moan, barely aware of the door closing behind me.

Vance's tongue pushes into my mouth, and just like a week ago when we kissed, I can't get enough. I don't even breathe because all my energy is going into tasting and exploring his mouth.

But I want more than just his mouth this time.

Vance slides his hands under my jacket, slipping it off my shoulders.

I go for his T-shirt, but he stops me.

Pulling back, I open my eyes and stare up at him. I might even be pouting. "Why'd you stop?"

"Because we have all night, and I want to feed you first."

"Feed ..." That's when I smell the most amazing things I've ever smelled. "Garlic and pasta sauce."

"Good nose. Hope you're hungry."

"Starving." I step closer to him. "But not for food."

Vance slumps against me, his hand around my back pulling me to him, and rests his head on my shoulder. "I'm trying to do the right thing here, but you're making it so hard."

"That makes two of us." I push my hips against his so he can feel my cock.

"Not that."

I pull back. "Wait, *not that*?"

"Well, yes, that too, but I want to do this the right way. Date you. Feed you."

"You don't need to wine and dine me to sixty-nine me."

Vance bursts out laughing, but he steps back. Away from me.

166

I don't like it.

I do, however, like it when his deep blue eyes meet mine, and he says, "You wanted to know if this was a last-man-on-Earth situation. That I found out you were interested and this is some kind of settling for what I can get type thing. I'm trying to prove to you that this isn't only about sex. Maybe it's not dating and won't go anywhere after we've gotten our fill, but I want you to know that it's at least more than settling. Because you deserve better than feeling like a consolation prize. You deserve to be looked at how every single player in the NHL looks at the Stanley Cup."

I blink. And then blink again. "That ... might possibly be the most romantic thing anyone's ever said to me, and all it's done is make me want to go to bed even more."

"You don't have much patience, do you?"

I step closer to him, close enough to pull him against me. "One, I'm a hockey player. We're not known for our patience. Two, I haven't been laid in ... math I can't even do. And three, I have wanted this since basically the moment I met you. Tell me, how am I supposed to be patient when it comes to that?"

"I'll turn the oven down to keep the food warm," he growls. "Get upstairs now."

"Which is your room?"

"The only one with a bed in it. Unless you want to fuck in the home gym."

"Eww, no. You'll probably make me stretch my adductor first."

He looks me over. "It's not the worst idea."

"I'm shutting my mouth now."

"Good. You better be naked and on my bed by the time I join you." Vance slaps my ass as I pass him, and that only makes me run up the stairs.

His room is decorated in warm tones and is fairly basic, but I don't slow down to take it all in. I'm too busy throwing my clothes all over the place as I struggle out of them.

I don't know why the second I'm naked, nerves kick in. He's seen me naked before. I've seen him naked. I've seen him play with his damn hole. It was through a screen, but still.

This shouldn't make me nervous, but it does.

Because it's happening.

It's Vance.

And maybe that's too much for my small little brain to comprehend.

It's not too much for my cock though. It already aches.

His voice travels from the doorway. "You look so hot naked."

I flinch because I didn't hear him come up the stairs.

"Did I scare you? Were you expecting someone else?"

I turn to him, putting my hands on my hips and not even caring that my cock is standing at attention and trying to wave hello to him. He's naked too, and oh, look at that, his cock is trying to wave back. "I didn't hear you come upstairs. You're all stealthy and shit."

"Or maybe …" He steps closer. "You were too in your head that you missed it. I wasn't exactly light-footed when I bolted up here to get to you."

Now my feet move in, closing most of the gap between us. "Bolted, huh?"

"There was definitely some bolting."

"There might have been some nerves," I admit.

"Second thoughts?"

"Fuck no. Never. I guess …" Maybe I don't want to tell him the truth. "Never mind. I'm fine."

"Oh, you are so not doing that to me. You guess what?" His naked torso presses against mine, our cocks meeting between us.

I'm already leaking, and I'm worried even the lightest touch will make me come.

Our breaths mingle. His forehead comes down on mine.

"I guess …" I swallow hard. "I guess I'm worried about what happens tomorrow. What happens if I've built you up in my head or that I've been so blinded by lust that once we do this, once you've made me come, that … everything changes?"

"I hope everything fucking changes," he murmurs.

I lift my head to look him in the eyes. "What?"

His lips twitch. "I hope they change for the better. I hope I can fulfill every fantasy you've ever had of me and that we can create new ones of our own. And if tomorrow you wake up repulsed by me, let me know. We might not know what we have yet, but we can't figure it out if we don't do some *experimenting*."

"You have the best answer for everything."

"I'm very wise." He nods solemnly.

"Wise? I dunno. You've been up here at least a couple of minutes, and I don't have a dick in my ass or my mouth yet, so how smart can you be?"

Vance shakes his head. "How are you the same guy that couldn't even pronounce 'perfect' in front of me not that long ago?"

"Do dirty words shock you?"

"Only coming from this mouth that I've thought was so innocent up until now." His thumb crosses over my bottom lip.

"My mouth is anything but innocent. Let me show you."

To put us both out of our misery, I sink to my knees.

CHAPTER TWENTY

VANCE

Plans be damned, this is a much, much better use of our time. Ayri Quinn on his knees for me almost makes me short-circuit, but then he wraps those pretty lips around my cock, and my entire body flares to life again.

For someone who hasn't been with another man in a long time, he hasn't lost his touch. He's right. There's nothing innocent about the way he's sucking my cock like a starved man.

He hums as he bobs up and down, pulling almost all the way off before sinking down as low as he can go. My cock is in warm, wet heaven. I'd had good intentions of making Quinn feel valued and secure, but look at how easily he derails my carefully laid plans.

I reach down to run my fingers through his hair, and his eyes flutter at the contact. He's a fucking dream. His mouth is going to wreck me.

Normally, I'm the kind of guy to bring a hookup home, we both get off, and then they're out the door before our cum has a chance to dry, and it's never occurred to me to care before. Transactional sex has suited me just fine because I've gotten what I needed out of it, but while I was cooking for Quinn, I got nervous to see him, and I liked it. I liked the thought of kissing him, and serving him up dinner, and spending time together before having what I'm convinced will be mind-blowing sex. It's going to happen out of the order I'd planned, but I'm still excited for it all.

Maybe I've been needing more for a while and never realized it.

He's so eager, hand steady on my ass to get a good pace going, while his other cups my balls. I could easily come like this, and soon, but while the timeline for tonight is out the window, my main priority isn't: looking after him and making him feel amazing.

I pull back, and he tries to follow my cock with his mouth, but I grip his jaw instead. "Up."

He pushes to his feet, breathing off rhythm and pupils blown out wide. My gaze runs greedily over his face before I pull him against me and kiss him again. Quinn's so responsive, so hungry for more, his tongue fights mine as I back us both toward the bed.

His thighs hit the mattress, and he falls onto it, moving backward further up the bed before I drag the flat of my tongue from his mouthwatering abs to his nipple and then settle over the top of him.

Quinn moans and wraps his arms around me, all that bare skin hot and flush against mine.

"Hi," I say, smiling down at him.

"Don't be cute. Just fuck me."

"Don't be desperate. Just enjoy yourself."

"Can't I do both?"

I pretend to think about it for a second, but I just can't. This is too much. I'm buzzing and aching, and seeing Quinn's smiling, turned-on face makes me drop my face to his shoulder again. I can't do it. I can't look at him. That face makes me want to give in to everything he asks for.

I kiss my way along his collarbone, suck on his shoulder, then make my way back up to his lips. We kiss slowly and deeply as I lazily grind my hips down into his. The intimate way our cocks slide together fills me with anticipation and need. Until Quinn squirms under me.

I pull back to find his lips swollen and red, his eyes wild. "Please. I need it."

"Need what?"

"You inside me."

I groan at how desperate he sounds. "Were you a good boy in the shower?"

"I did everything. I'm all ready."

An image of Quinn working himself open flashes before my eyes and has me scrambling for the lube and condom I optimistically stashed under my pillow earlier. "You have no idea how hot that makes me."

"Yeah?"

"Mhmm. I might have to watch one day."

He grins, that rare confidence flickering through as he takes the lube from me. "Why not right now?"

"Oh, fuck." My eyes are locked on his movements as he rubs lube over his fingers. Then he pulls his legs open, and I push up to kneel between them. He wasn't lying when he said he was ready. I watch as he slides two fingers into his hole, body opening easily around him. He fucks himself on them for a couple of minutes, knees pulled back, mouth open and panting, flushed from cheeks to chest in a glorious shade of red.

I grunt, then lean down and flick my tongue around his stretched rim. His fingers stall, body shuddering, and I hurry to tear open the condom and roll it down my shaft.

"Ready to show me how good you are at taking a cock?"

"Fuck yes," he rasps.

I grab his firm, round glutes and hold them open, cock throbbing at the sight of him fingering himself. "Put me in, then."

His fingers disappear from his ass, leaving him red and open as he grabs the lube and squeezes a generous amount over my cockhead.

Quinn strokes it over my length as he guides my tip to his hole. "Needed this … so long …"

"Then take it."

He bears down, grip tightening on my shaft as his body opens around me and sucks me in. The second my tip is swallowed, Quinn releases my dick and grabs my ass, controlling the speed I enter him.

My hands are braced on either side of him on the bed, holding myself back from taking over. What I want more than anything is to give him what he needs, and while I'm desperate to slam home, my gaze stays locked on this gorgeous, stubborn man as he takes exactly what he wants from me.

The second I'm fully seated, Quinn's hands slip from my ass up my back, and he pulls me to him.

"H-hi."

I huff a laugh. "Now who's being cute?"

"Can't help it," he says, voice deep and husky. "This is actually happening."

The awe in his voice hits me straight in the chest, and I give him a soft smile before taking his mouth again. I hook my arm under one of his knees and pull his leg up onto my shoulder as I grind deep inside him.

The heat and pressure surrounding me has my body alight. We make out, bodies writhing together for who knows how long. I forget about time and dinner and everything else other than how Quinn's mouth and ass feel consuming me. We move together for so long my cock almost hurts from how worked up it is. I'm edging myself, holding back, sinking into feeling and nothing else.

His hands don't stop moving. From my ass to my chest to my back. He cups my face and pulls my hair and squirms beneath me. Between kisses, he moans my name and curses and whines at me that he needs more. His cock has left a sticky mess between us that I want to lick up once we're done.

"Fuck me, Vance," he rasps.

"But I'm having so much fun dragging this out," I tease.

Apparently, that's the wrong answer because Quinn throws me off him. Nothing but apologies are about

175

to leave my mouth when he tackles me onto my back, straddles my waist, and sinks down onto me.

Then I have the most amazing view of Ayri Quinn fucking himself on my cock. His powerful thighs work him up and down, ass slapping against my hips, hands braced on my chest, and his blunt nails digging into my skin. I wanted him to take what he wanted, and he's doing it. Unapologetically. His grunts fill my room, and I can barely catch my breath as I take his hips and meet his rhythm. We're in a frenzied race to the end, head-board banging against the wall. A line of sweat runs down Quinn's throat, and I desperately want to lean up and follow it with my tongue.

"Tell me you're close," I beg.

He nods, not able to form words, and when the pressure in my balls gets too tight, when I'm so close I can almost taste my orgasm, I close my hand around his cock and jerk him off.

Quinn cries out and comes, and this time, I watch the whole thing. Feel his dick pulse in my hand, the way his breath catches, holds, releases, before he covers me in his cum.

I grab him and roll him beneath me again, smearing the mess between us, and shove back into his ass. I pound into him, chasing the edge, body so tight and ready for pleasure that when it slams into me, I just hold him close and ride out the waves as my cock throbs deep inside him.

We're both a sweaty, cummy mess by the time I'm able to catch my breath again, and when I look down at him, I find him already directing a soft look my way.

"Wow," he whispers.

I kiss his jaw and hum. "Didn't disappoint?"

"I underestimated you. Which, considering how horny for me Fantasy You is, I wouldn't have thought that was possible."

I laugh and rest my cheek on his chest. "I don't wanna let you go yet."

"What about dinner?"

"You hockey players are always thinking about food."

"Sex and food. You're the one who promised to feed me, and I already got the sex part."

"Because you're the stubborn one who wanted to get off first." I smile against his pec, too sleepy and wrung out to move.

"We could shower first …"

That gets my attention. I prop up on my elbows. "Shower, then you'll *finally* let me give you a proper date."

"Finally?" He laughs. "You say that like you're the one who's waited forever for this."

"Forever. One night. Same thing, right?"

"I don't think lady parts were the only thing you failed in college."

I snigger and pull out of him before offering him a hand up. When he's sitting face-to-face with me, noses almost touching, I can't help but lean in and brush my lips over his.

"Tell me you'll stay tonight?"

"Tonight?" Confusion crosses his face. "What happened to two days?"

And somehow, that's the best answer he could have given me.

CHAPTER TWENTY-ONE

QUINN

Considering what we just did, I don't know why I blush when Vance puts a bowl of spaghetti in front of me and kisses the top of my head.

He disappears back into the kitchen and returns with a bottle of red.

"None for me," I say when he goes to pour me a glass. "I'm already going to have to put in double the time in the gym tomorrow if I eat all of this pasta."

Vance clucks his tongue. "One glass won't hurt your fitness, and no, you won't. It's zucchini, not pasta. Ground chicken breast, not beef. The worst thing in there is the tiny bit of sugar I added to the sauce."

I lean in, inspecting Vance's cooking skills because damn. "In that case, fill me up."

"Don't get too excited." He finishes pouring the glass of wine and then sits at the head of the table to my side. "It doesn't taste like proper spaghetti."

"I'm used to food not tasting like food."

Vance laughs. "It's still food."

"I stand by my statement." I twist my fork into the zucchini noodles and stuff it in my mouth. The flavor of the sauce bursts on my tongue. "Damn. Maybe I stand corrected. This is awesome. Good at cooking and sex. You're a triple threat."

"Cooking and sex are only two things."

I shake my head and take a sip of wine to wash down the food I'm practically inhaling. "Not the way you do sex. You get two points for that."

The smile on Vance's face makes me think I've either said something really wrong or really right. "Glad I didn't crack under all that pressure you put me under."

"Nah, I had faith. Well, no, I had faith that you turn me on so much just by being in the same room as me that it wasn't going to take me much to come."

Vance taps his chin. "Only question is, should I use this superpower for good or for evil?"

"Always evil." Then I think about my answer. "Wait, no. Use it whenever you want except at work."

Vance licks his lips and takes another sip of wine. "We're probably going to have to do something about that."

I stop chewing and lift the hem of my shirt to wipe my face. "About your superpower?"

"About work, you slob." He hands me a napkin.

"Eh. My shirt will do."

"Sometimes I forget how young you are."

"Twenty-four isn't young. Especially in hockey."

"Bullshit. You're in your prime. You've got enough experience to know what you're doing out there while still being young enough that you don't need knee or hip replacements yet."

"Ah, the things I have to look forward to. I guess we're just going to have to make good use of my knees while they still work."

Vance throws his head back. "Yup. Definitely going to have to do something about work."

"What about it?"

"I'm not saying we need to tell everyone or anything, but we should probably tell the people who need to know. Like Boone. The GM. Just to cover the organization."

"What, in case it all blows up?" Like he's already preparing for when he's done with me.

"Not like that. But, okay, just say we keep this a secret. We see each other whenever we can outside of work, no sharing rooms on road trips or anything like that, but we get sloppy. Someone sees us. They misinterpret it, and suddenly, they're telling people they saw you in a compromising position with me and it didn't look consensual or something. It's to protect both of us and the club from issues when it does get out."

"When it gets out," I murmur.

"I think it's inevitable at this point. I can't look at you anymore without thinking about how sexy you looked under me. Unless I'm being presumptuous and you're currently thinking about the best way to get out of here?"

"Fuck no." He really is giving this a go. Us. Whatever it may or may not grow into. This time when I blush, it's not because I'm reliving the sex in my head. It's because

I'm starting to believe him. That we could have something real.

He's said it, but with how undeniably awkward I've been around him in the past, I guess I didn't truly believe it until now, when he's putting his career on the line by telling management.

I just hope they take it better than San Jose did when they found out Oskar was having a thing with Lane—the team's PR manager.

"We should tell management," I say. "But if they fire you—"

"They won't. They'll probably get us to sign something saying we won't sue the organization if we break up and a declaration saying we're entering into this voluntarily."

"Really, all they'd have to do is take one look at how hot you are and know it's voluntary." Still, telling management makes it official, and this is still so new. What if Vance goes through all this and then decides I'm not worth it? He wouldn't be the first guy to think that.

Vance chuckles. "Is that … charm coming out of your mouth?"

"Charm, buttering you up so that when I ask for more fake pasta, you'll load up my plate … same thing."

"On it." He brings the pan the spaghetti's resting in and dumps more into my bowl before returning it to the kitchen.

I've noticed he's hardly touched his. "Not hungry?"

"I'm waiting to see if you'll ask to eat mine too." He smirks. "But no, I was munching while I was cooking." Still, he takes a forkful and scoops it into his mouth.

For what I'd consider a first date, it's … kinda perfect. It's casual, I got off before the dinner part, and now we can just hang out.

"What should we do on your days off other than make sure you do your weights?" he asks.

"Not even leave the bed?"

"As amazing as that plan sounds, I thought we could go out. Do something. Somewhere. What do you usually do on your days off?"

"Sleep. Watch TV. Annoy Asher."

"Okay, none of those count as bridges. We have to find you your bridges."

I put my fork down. "I asked the Collective about that. How you pointed out I don't have anything outside of hockey. And they said their things were sex—"

"Doesn't count, but go on."

"Volunteering for a charity or coaching."

Vance rubs his chin. "How do you feel about waterfalls? We live right near one of the most famous waterfalls in the world."

"You know what that old song says. You shouldn't chase them. But also, I've been to Niagara a million times and had no interest. Yeah, it's pretty, but could I see myself staring at it for hours? No."

"Arcade games?"

I make a buzzer sound.

"Art museums?"

"Do I look like I'm the kind of person who knows art?"

Vance shrugs. "You don't have to know it. Just have to like it."

"Nope."

He leans back in his seat. "Where do you get your stubborn streak from?"

"I'm not stubborn."

"Uh-huh. Sure. You're only about as stubborn as you are gay."

"Yeah? Well, you're as good-looking as you are annoying. How about that?"

"So glad we have come to the mature part of the evening."

I'm tempted to stick my tongue out at him, but that would only be proving his point.

"I think I have something you might like to do," Vance says.

"I *know* you have something I'd like to do. And just did." I flick my gaze to his crotch and back up again.

"Sex doesn't count as a non-hockey thing."

"Why not?"

"Because when the only other thing in your life is sex, going out to get it after a bad night on the ice is a slippery slope into forming another bad habit."

I cock my head. "Another? What was my first?"

"Workaholic."

"I'm not a workaholic. I'm a hockeyaholic."

"Which for you is work. Ergo—"

"Ergo no, I'm not."

Vance just smiles again, that look that sits somewhere between him thinking I'm cute but also a dumbass. "Tell me that thing about not being stubborn again."

I sigh. "Fine. I give in. I'll do your thing that's not sex or hockey related. Or bridge related."

"I promise it's not sex or hockey related, but it could be bridge related."

I narrow my gaze. "You know I'm not allowed to go bungee jumping or any of those other extreme sports, right? My body is a temple."

"I'll worship your body again later. Right now, I have some planning to do." He stands from the table.

"Wait, what am I going to do while you're planning?"

"You could always do the dishes."

"How did I ever get so lucky?" I deadpan.

He blinks at me like I'm being serious.

"I'm joking. You cooked, I'll clean. Fair's fair."

"You know what would be really fair?"

"What?"

"If after I do up this plan, you have a turn of my ass."

I stand in a hurry and start collecting plates. "Question, does throwing all your dishes out count as doing them? I'll buy you new ones."

Vance comes up behind me and takes hold of my shoulders to steer me toward the kitchen. "Take your time. I have to look up some things."

"Okay, if it's not bungee jumping but involves bridges—"

"Could possibly involve bridges. I didn't say definitely."

I am so confused. "Where the hell are you taking me?"

—

"Let's start with coffee and breakfast." Vance has way too much pep in his step for this time of morning. He has a backpack and bottled water and is layered up to brave the cold.

"You woke me up. On my day off. For coffee and what I'm assuming is a hike with the way you're dressed."

"You're cranky in the mornings." Vance throws his arm around my shoulders, not caring who on the street sees the PDA. I can only think it's because we have plans to tell team management, but I hope we're not caught before then.

"Should you be doing that if we haven't told Boone yet?"

He keeps his arm around me. "Who says I haven't? I sent him a text last night."

"Saying we're sleeping together?" I shriek.

"No. That we need to set up a time to talk to him and the GM. He replied asking if it had to do with what he thinks it has to do with, and I said yes. So, it's more or less done. We just need to get a meeting time to do it officially."

"Oh." I take my phone out of my pocket. "I'm surprised my phone isn't blowing up yet."

"It's not official yet." We head toward the baseball field and stop by a coffee shop in one of the business buildings nearby for breakfast.

We get it to go and eat and drink while we walk, but I still have no idea what we're doing. "Walking tour of the city?" I guess.

"Kind of."

"Going to try to convince me to switch to baseball?" I ask as we get to the stadium.

"Yup. That's it. Come on, this way." He takes me into a parking garage, of all places, and tells me to keep a lookout for a box.

"A box?"

"Yup. Something with maybe this logo on it." He shows me his screen.

"Is this some secret society shit?"

He laughs. "Kind of."

"Is that your answer to everything I ask?"

"Kind of."

"Smartass."

"What, like you're the only one who's allowed to be snarky?"

"Yes. The younger person in the couple always gets to be the snarky one."

He presses his lips together to think about that. "Didn't I read somewhere that Ezra is older than Anton?"

"By one year. Doesn't count."

"Hmm. Maybe. Okay, I don't think it's going to be in the building. We should go back and look at the entrance."

I follow him but am only getting more and more frustrated as I do. "What the hell are we doing here?"

"Ah-ha!" He picks up a small box that he finds in ... a tree lining the street.

"What … What is that?"

He smiles widely. "It's our cache."

"Our what?"

"We're geocaching, baby." He opens the box, pulls out a pen and paper, and writes down our initials on a list.

"What the fuck is geocaching?"

"So there are these boxes hidden all over the city, right? All over the world. People have to track them down via the app, and then they leave something." He pulls out a Buffalo hockey key ring and chucks it into the box. "And take something." He passes me a tiny troll doll that looks like it came from the eighties or nineties. It's dirty, the hair is almost nonexistent, and it's creepy as fuck.

"What else is in there?" I look, and it's all junk, but the idea is cool. "So these are hidden anywhere?"

"Anywhere."

"All over the world?"

"Yep."

"That's …"

"Let me guess, you hate this too?"

I twirl the ugly-ass troll around my fingers. "Fuck no. Let's go find them all!"

Vance lets out a loud, relieved breath. "Good. I was starting to think you were an alien sent to Earth to study hockey and nothing else."

"Where's the next one? I'll race you!" I steal his phone.

Before I can run off, I hear him mutter, "What have I done?"

CHAPTER TWENTY-TWO

VANCE

I didn't realize how stressed I was about this whole meeting until I'm stepping out of Pete Gavin's office. Our meeting with the GM went better than I thought it would, and as soon as we're in the clear, I turn my attention to Boone.

"That's it?"

"I might have, ah, given him the heads-up. Gavin's getting old, Vance. No need to give the man a heart attack."

I give him a wry smile. "A heart attack over us dating or men dating?"

"As far as GMs go, he's a good one. He only cares about talent, even if personally, he doesn't"—Boone uses air quotes—"'get' the gay thing. Your job will never be in jeopardy because of it."

And while I still don't view that as being any shade of acceptable, he's right. There are teams out there that would have turned their backs on Dalton and Quinn the second they walked into the locker room. It sucks that we're still expected to be grateful for the scraps.

"You're thinking too deep over there," Quinn says, warm hand sliding into mine as we make our way back downstairs.

It makes me feel lighter as I realize we're doing this. We've signed the paperwork we needed to sign, management isn't going to be a problem, and now we're free to work out whatever we are without the outside pressure of keeping it a secret.

"I'm glad you two are happy," Boone says. "But I've gotta say one thing, and you won't hear more from me. The team is important to you both. Management is fine with things now, but they won't be if there's drama. If what you have is just physical, I'd urge you to think about whether being together is the right choice. If there's real feelings, that's something I fully support exploring. I just don't want to see either of you boys hurt. It's a stressful enough industry as it is."

And while his warning is about a step behind where I'm at, I appreciate the concern.

"Aww, you big softie," I tease, slinging an arm around his shoulders and pulling him in for a quick side hug. "But you don't need to worry. This is new, but it's something."

"New for you, maybe," Quinn says under his breath.

"What about the team?" Boone asks.

Quinn surprises me by answering first. "Asher already knows, but I don't want the rest finding out yet. First, it's a lot of pressure when we're figuring things out, and second, we're having a great season, so I don't want anything to get in their heads and throw us off. I've done that enough this season."

"And you've blamed yourself enough too, so quit it." I give him a playful tap on the back of the head.

"I've changed my mind. I don't like you anymore."

"You say that to me at least once a day."

"That's because you call me on my shit at least once a day."

"And *that's* because you make it so easy to."

Boone sniggers. "Yeah, good luck keeping this all quiet from the team."

"We're pretty stealthy," Quinn says.

"Right. Everything you've done this far supports that."

"Hey," Quinn says. "I've had a crush on Vance for a year, and no one knew."

Boone actually tosses his head back as he laughs. "Everyone knew." He slaps my shoulder. "Except this guy."

Quinn's cheeks rapidly turn red, and I step closer and pull him to me.

"For what it's worth, we've already established I'm a dumbass. And you're adorable."

"And that stache has still gotta go," Boone cuts in.

"Maybe it's the start of his playoff beard," I say right before Quinn's palm slaps over my mouth.

"Are you *trying* to jinx us?"

"I'm must mat comfiment."

"I don't care what that bumbling was. We're pretending it didn't happen." He moves his palm.

"Speaking of hockey and things we're not talking about." Boone plants his hands on his hips. "You had some good wins while you were away."

"I did." Quinn's eyes flick to mine. "I'm working on it. I want back on Asher's line."

"Dalton wants that too," I say. "He keeps calling Ducre Quinn Junior. I think Ducre is ready to stab him with his skate."

"Asher has that effect on people," Quinn says.

And like we've summoned the guy himself, a door down the end of the hall slams open, and in he walks. His gym bag is over one shoulder, and he barely spares the three of us a glance as he passes on his way to the weight room.

"Is it just me, or was Dalton Dalton-ing harder than usual?" I ask.

Quinn sighs. "My guesses are either Ezra's in town—"

"Boston is playing Colorado tonight—"

"Or he's missing Kole."

"His boyfriend?" I clarify. Because the thought of Dalton missing anyone blows my mind. It's hard to remember the guy has actual feelings.

"Yeah. The longer they go not seeing each other, the harder he takes it."

"Why's he here?" Boone asks. "You've still got today off. I didn't think I'd see him around."

A gorgeous smile crosses Quinn's face. "PR training. Coach is putting a stop to the *eat shit and die* responses."

"I'm surprised no one has stepped in sooner, but a lot of the time, those reporters are hounding him for that kind of response. Constantly being reminded of his brother's rookie stats wouldn't be easy when he's having the kind of rookie year most players dream of," Boone says.

"Well, while he works on that, we have weight training to do back at home," I say, taking Quinn's hand to drag him away.

Boone lifts a hand. "Don't need to know."

"I mean *actual* weight training."

Quinn screws up his face, but when Boone splits off to his offices, I lean in and whisper, "With lots of blowjobs to reward you."

Our two days off together pass too quickly. Between the meeting, geocaching, weights, and sex, we eat and hang out in front of the TV. Being lazy isn't something I'm used to; forgetting about work and what's going on with the team is completely foreign to me. But then Quinn's there with his stories about the Collective, and his naked skin, and the way he blushes, and he makes it nearly impossible to think about anything else.

He stretches out beside me in bed. We both have to get up and get ready in about ten minutes, but that would mean letting go of his waist, and I really don't wanna.

"I'm nervous about tonight," he says softly.

"Hmm. Why?"

"We're getting to the point of the season where I'm running out of chances to make a comeback. If I can't prove my worth in the next two months, I'm just going to be the guy who coasted by on his team's hard work."

"You're putting unnecessary pressure on yourself by looking at it that way."

"I know." His defeated tone tells me he's not going to stop though. I get the impression he doesn't think he can stop that train of thought.

"Why do you think you need to make a comeback?"

"I can't tell if you're asking stupid questions on purpose or not."

I laugh and kiss his shoulder. "Why can't you aim to have a good game *tonight*? Focus on *one* game without losing the puck. *One* game with no sloppy penalties. You're too busy looking at the end game to focus on where to start."

He groans. "That sounds so rookie."

"What's wrong with that?"

"This is my *third* season in the NHL. I should know what I'm doing by now."

"You do know what you're supposed to be doing. Which is why you're frustrated that you're not doing it. Take a step back, and be kinder to yourself."

He humphs.

"And if that doesn't work, do it for me."

Quinn's eyes are more gold in the morning sun, and when he glances at me, they're filled with amusement. "Shouldn't you be telling me to do it for myself?"

"Yeah, clearly, that's not working. So until you *want* to do it for yourself, do it for me. I dare you. I dare you to go out there and prove to me that you know how to strip a puck. That you know how to control your stops. I dare you to prove to me that you can get through a game with no penalties or sloppy passes."

He grins. "Not going to ask me to score for you too?"

"Nope. I don't even want you to think about scoring."

"I don't think you know how hockey works."

I laugh and bury my face in his neck. "All I want from you tonight is to walk away happy. Remember why you love the game. Be confident that you played well enough that it's a good stepping point for the next game."

"Mmm, talk dirty to me," he says dryly.

"And if you do that, I'll spend the rest of the night eating your ass."

Quinn throws off the covers and jumps out of bed. I'm surprised he's rocking a semi when his last orgasm wasn't even half an hour ago, but he hops around, pulling on his briefs. "Deal. I'm going to play the most baseline, average, unremarkable, and safe game of my life."

Yeah, I'll believe that when I see it.

He immediately stops, face falling. "Fuck. We're playing Seattle."

"Yeah?"

"That means I have to meet up with Aleks after. Collective rules."

"Are you saying Collective rules, like 'woo, the Collective rules, high five!' or 'these are the rules set by the Collective'? Because the first one is a little too high school for me to handle."

He shakes his head. "The second. Definitely. Though when I say Collective rules, I more mean rules set forth by Ezra Palaszczuk that we all appreciate though only follow to the letter to avoid him sulking and being *extra* Ezra-ish the next time we see him."

"Yikes. Normal Ezra seems like enough to handle for me."

Quinn turns those gorgeous eyes on me. "Will you come?"

"Again? Geez, it's barely been—"

"*No.*" He tugs his bottom lip between his teeth. "Tonight. Out of everyone, Aleks is probably the most low-key to meet first. Or ... I should say again. You met him the night I first injured myself."

"I-I know who Aleksander Emerson is." I'm not totally sure my mouth isn't hanging open though. "You ... want me to meet your friends as me? Like, you and me, not team trainer me?"

"If it's too early, I totally understand. No. It's definitely too early. It is, right? Forget I said anything. There's no hurry. I'm not used to the whole relationship thing, and sometimes I don't think and *blerg* comes out of my mouth, and we can just ignore everything up until this moment right before I started rambling and can't switch off."

I climb out of bed and pull him in close. That at least dries up all the words, and he sags against me.

"I hate myself."

I hold him tighter, smiling into his hair. "I love the rambling. As for your friends, I definitely want to meet them. Officially. Let's see how tonight goes though. I don't want to encroach on your time with them, and we're still playing this low-key. That's not me saying no, because it means a lot that you asked, just me saying to take the day to think about it."

"There you go being wise again."

I kiss his forehead and let him go. "And my next wise-ism: I'm going to shower first and head in. You give it a bit of time, and lock up behind you as you leave."

"*Urgh*, I hate that."

"Me too, but your points were all valid."

"Can we just forget my points and have shower sex instead?"

"Nope, but I appreciate the offer."

Once I'm done showering, he's still in his briefs, sitting on the edge of my bed and scrolling through his phone.

"I'll see you in there," I say.

"One good thing about our relationship is that if I'm fired for playing so shit, it means more time spent having sex."

"Downside to that is I'm not a multimillionaire, so I still have to work."

"I could pay you to be my sex master."

I laugh. "Why don't we work on becoming boyfriends and you *not* losing your job? That can be plan B."

"Boyfriends, huh?" The lopsided smile he sends my way makes me wish we could spend another day in bed too.

"Isn't that what we're working on?"

"Yeah, I just didn't think about it that deeply. Kinda hard to think about anything after a two-day fuck fest."

"Stop trying to distract me with more sex. I'll see you at work." I pause on my way out the door. "Good luck tonight. O'Hennessy's on this game, but I'll be watching."

"Yeah?"

I try to hold back my amusement. "Turns out there's this player I've always loved watching on the ice. Because of his skill and the way he plays. No other reason."

"If you're talking about Asher—"

"Nope, no joking. He's got nothing on you, Ayri. And I can't wait to see the game where you remember that."

CHAPTER TWENTY-THREE

QUINN

Every time doubt tries to creep into my thoughts during this game, I think of Vance's words. Do this for him. Have a good game for him. Not for me.

The mantra is working so far, and I managed to put one in the net in the first period, get an assist in this one, but it's now nearing the end of the second, and everything in me is starting to wane.

I'm currently off, sitting on the team bench and watching as we hold on to a very tight lead. Being on the fourth line now, my ice time is limited, so if I'm going to get out there to prove myself, I only have precious minutes to do it.

I shake my head, and sweat rolls down the side of my face as I remind myself this game isn't for me.

My only focus should be showing Vance what I can do, and fuck do I want him to see how truly amazing I can be out there.

Coach sends me back on, and instead of concentrating on what I should be doing, I distract my invasive need-to thoughts with Vance. Vance naked. All his muscles. His cock. The way he kisses so forcefully and knowing I can have that as soon as this game is over. As soon as I show Vance that I can be confident. I know how to score, and later, I'll be scoring on him.

By some miracle, because the distractions might be working so well I'm no longer keeping my eye on the puck, I get possession and see an opening in Seattle's defense.

For the first time since maybe my injury, I'm not cautious. I don't play it safe. There's absolutely no hesitation as I fly down the ice, my blades carrying me at crazy speed through the hole the two Seattle defensemen have left for me. I make it past them, deke out the goalie, making him think I'll shoot from my left, but with quick feet, I turn, take my shot, and send the puck soaring to the top right of the net.

My linemates jump on me when the lamp lights up for the second time for me tonight.

That stokes a fire under my ass, and that invincible feeling that I haven't had in so long fills my veins.

I'm not worried about checks; I bulldoze, zigzag, and skate circles around the other team, and I'm buzzing.

Coach keeps me and my line out there for the last few minutes of the second period, making it my longest shift since before All-Stars.

The team heads down the chute, and as I pass the stands where a lot of the team get their comped seats, my face falls because Vance isn't where he was during the first period. Did I do all of that for him and he wasn't even watching?

My hyper mood just as quickly becomes somber. That is, until I enter the locker room to find Vance next to O'Hennessy outside the treatment room, and it perks right back up again.

He beams at me, and Boone's right. There's no way the team won't know something's up if we can't stop looking at each other with goofy grins on our faces.

Müller is first in the treatment room to change over a bandage from a face scratch he got in the first period from Aleks's stick, which I'll totally be bringing up with him after the game.

Surprising me, Vance approaches as I sit at my cubby and pour water down my throat.

He stands above me, way too sexy not to stare at his crotch, which is at my eye level, so it's not even my fault. But then he kneels. "How's the groin strain?"

I want to say *hard, thanks to you*, but I don't. "Feeling good." *Would be better if you gave it a rub.*

Yeah, I don't see how Vance and I can keep it professional anymore.

"Make sure you go see O'Hennessy if that changes."

I nod, and he stands again to give Coach space to give us his third-period speech. The *we're doing great* and *almost at the finish line, so don't slack off now* speech.

Next to me, Asher's smirking in my direction.

"Only a matter of time until everyone finds out," he sings.

I nudge him hard.

He throws his hands up. "Hey, if anyone does find out, you can't blame me. You have to stop drooling over him."

"Eh. According to Boone, everyone knows about my crush anyway."

Müller joins us with a fresh butterfly bandage on his chin. "Crush? Oh, on Vance? Yeah, it's true. Everyone knows about it." He puts his hand on my shoulder. "He's way out of your league, by the way."

Asher snorts.

"He wouldn't be," Müller adds, "if you got rid of the pubes growing out your nose."

"Ah. More stache jokes. Brilliant. Bring them on." I fold my arms.

"Nice lipholstry," Asher says.

I turn my head toward him. "How long you been holding on to that one?"

"A while."

I laugh. "I like it."

"I think you've misplaced your eyebrow," Müller says.

"Fuck off."

We all laugh, but it's cut off by Coach asking if we've got our heads in the game or up our asses.

"If I had the ability to put my head up my ass, I'd never get any work done," Asher says.

The team snickers, and I swear even Coach's lips twitch, but if Asher continues to go down this path of talking back to our coaches, reporters, and fans, I worry about his longevity in this sport. Or … as a functioning human in society, really.

We're sent back on the ice, and I'm almost disappointed for the break because I was on a hot streak before the buzzer went off, and now I need to go out there and follow it up. It takes a bit to warm up again, to get back into that mode and not the overthinking headspace, but when I do, everything clicks. I'm making passes, outskating everyone else, and I think I've taken more shots on goal this period than I have in the last six games. None of them go in, but it really feels like I'm back.

I'm me again.

After we get called back in and the first line goes out, Coach taps me on the shoulder.

"Quinn, Ducre, next shift, you're swapping places."

And just like that, I get my spot back on third line.

Sorry, not sorry, Rook.

-

Vance and Asher move about my kitchen, pouring drinks and getting out plates for the food we've got coming, talking about the game and acting like they're the best of friends. It's a bit of a surreal sight, but I'm happy Asher isn't giving Vance his usual grumpy front. He's not teasing us either about being together.

In fact, I can't think of the last time Asher was truly snarky to me other than all that mustache talk with Müller in the locker room.

I stop setting the table and turn to him. "You're happy."

"Me or Dalton?" Vance asks.

"Dalton."

"Fuck off, am not," he protests, but even that seems half-assed.

"You're really happy," I say. "Why?"

"No reason. Just ... am."

"I call bullshit. Asher eat-shit-and-die Dalton doesn't do happy unless it has something to do with Kole. Or his family. But not West. Just your billions of other siblings."

"That's not true at all."

I'm expecting him to dispute the whole thing I just said, saying he doesn't care about anything, but instead, he surprises me.

"I don't have any beef with West. We're good. It's the media that's trying to give us beef."

"Hmm," Vance cuts in. "Swearing at them when they ask about your brother probably only fuels them."

"Ugh, you sound exactly like the PR people."

Vance laughs.

I point at Asher. "Stop avoiding the question. If you have good news, you have to share with the class."

"It's nothing! Kole and I just had a good talk last night. That's all."

"Ah." I know where that's going. "Video sex."

I don't need to glance at Vance to know he's thinking about the first orgasms we shared over video call.

Asher shakes his head. "Nope. Even better than that. We had a massive talk about how long distance is sucking, and ... he's decided to do his residency here in Buffalo. There was talk about him trying to get into a residency program in Boston because apparently the programs there are so much better than here, but he's decided to come here. So ..." The look of complete love coming from

Asher still throws me sometimes, but I'm getting used to it.

Vance, however, is not. He stumbles back and grips the kitchen counter. "Asher Dalton is ... sweet?"

"He is. Little cinnamon roll."

That's when he gives us the double middle fingers. Right on time with the doorbell sounding.

"That'll be Aleks." I head for the door, but Aleks is not standing in front of me.

Kole is. "I thought he'd be here. He didn't know I was coming."

I step aside. "Heard you're moving to Buffalo."

Kole smiles as he passes me. "Yup. Eventually. I'm only here for one day, but I had to hop a plane to see him."

"That's so cute."

But he's not paying attention to me anymore. Asher comes running out of the kitchen and into the foyer. He only pauses for a second before he keeps on marching through.

"Sorry, can't stay for food." He takes Kole's hand and drags him out of the house.

They pass Aleks, who's on his way up to the house, but he's not alone.

"Bilson?" I ask with a confused scrunch in my brow.

"You have to save me," Cody Bilson, a winger for Seattle, cries.

Aleks looks like his supportive side is being tested. "He's being dramatic. He's on a celibacy kick right now, so he doesn't want to be where any women are."

Bilson covers his face. "Sex leads to marriage proposals, and my lawyer is sick of drawing up prenups for me."

Vance appears next to me, wrapping his arm around my waist. "What's happening?"

Aleks isn't surprised because he already knows about us, but Bilson cocks his head and says, "I know you. Where do I know you from?"

"Bilson, this is Vance. A trainer for Buffalo."

Bilson snaps his fingers. "Ah. That's it. So, how do we welcome me into this queer groupy thing?"

"We don't," Aleks says.

"You said queer spaces are safe spaces."

"For *queer* people," Aleks emphasizes.

"What do you have to do to qualify? Kiss a guy, suck a dick? I'll do anything. Just save me from all the women who tempt me."

I glance at Aleks. He shrugs at me.

"Come on in." *After all, if you're willing to have sex with a man to get away from women, you might be more queer than you realize.*

"Well, this should be fun," Vance says after Aleks and Bilson are inside.

"Fun is one word for it."

I say that, but as the night goes on, I realize I was definitely right having Vance meet Aleks first. He's much more down-to-earth than a lot of the other Collective guys.

Bilson, on the other hand … let's just say if he ever does cross over from heteroworld into bi-land, he'll fit in with the rest of the guys.

At one point, while Aleks is trying to confiscate Bilson's phone to stop him from going on Tinder and they're fighting it out, Vance leans in and whispers, "I like your friends."

If Vance can handle this, he'll be able to handle anything the rest of the Collective throws at him.

I think.

CHAPTER TWENTY-FOUR

VANCE

I catch Quinn on his way past the empty treatment room, and after checking Dalton is the only one around, I wrap my arm around Quinn's waist and yank him inside. His body hits mine, and I slam the door closed behind us before backing him into it.

"You need to stop doing that."

"Doing what?" he asks. So innocently. He's driving me crazy.

"Walking. Thinking. Existing in the same space as me." My lips skim his jaw. "You're making it a real effort in self-restraint to keep away from you."

He chuckles, gripping the front of my team trainer jacket. "Your self-restraint sucks."

"Want me to try harder?"

"Definitely not."

I smile as I bring our mouths together, and as soon as we're kissing, the desperation around me lifts. It's impossible to wrap my head around that when he injured himself, I had my hands on his body, turned him on, and never needed to act on the urge. But now that Quinn isn't off-limits? Now I'm allowed to touch him? Just being in the same room together is near impossible. When I see him, I want to fix his messy hair, feel the scrape of his mustache on my lips, hook my thumb into the band of his athletic shorts, and make sure everyone knows who gets to take him home at night.

Because every night he's in Buffalo, we're together. His place, my place, neither of us gives a shit. Not even for sex either. At a game last week, he took a hard hit to his knee that took him out of action for a day, but we just hung out talking, me icing his injury on and off, and Quinn didn't complain about being restricted once.

We've also been working more on his *thing*. Geocaching was a win, and I'm planning on taking him when we're in Boston next month, but we've also had a few video game nights, which went fine, tried reading, which was a huge miss for us both, and went volunteering at an animal shelter downtown. That one was good for us both, but not something we can do regularly with his schedule.

"I don't wanna leave tomorrow," he murmurs and kisses down my neck.

I know the feeling. I still have him pinned against the treatment room door, unwilling to let him go, even though I need to before someone comes knocking. "At least it's only three days this time."

He scowls. "Exactly. Three days. Three *whole* days. It's like you don't even care."

I laugh at his dramatics. "You'll be too busy kicking ass to care. Besides, it'll give us a chance to relive our first date."

Quinn perks up. "I like that idea."

"I thought you might." I pull away and run my hands through my hair. "You're not going to be happy with me tonight though."

"Why?"

"Because I forgot I told Joe I'd meet up with him. I already rescheduled on him last week."

"Ah. Joe. From college?"

"Get that jealous tone out of your mouth."

"Jealous? Me? No, not at all. Definitely not of some hot Joe who I've never met."

I'm smiling so wide it should be illegal. "Done yet?"

"Not sure."

"If you had let me finish before you got all cute, I thought ... since we can't head straight home, maybe you would, maybe, wanna come?"

His eyes snap up to mine. "Really?"

"Well, I met your friends. And I already mentioned you to him before anything happened between us, so he's been asking about you."

And look at that—now Quinn's smile should be illegal. "Yes. I'll come." He's bouncing up and down like a fucking puppy. "What time? Should I go home and change first?"

"Yes, because you know we can't leave here together." The slightest disappointment settles over that. "Change and be at my place at six. We'll head to the restaurant together."

Quinn screws up his face. "Six? Who has dinner that early?"

"People with children."

"Huh. Kids really do ruin everything, don't they?"

"Maybe don't use that as a conversation starter."

"Good point."

I give him one last kiss before kicking him out of the room. Müller's waiting, and he sends Quinn a not-so-subtle wink that makes me want to face-palm. The team might not know about us now, but I get the feeling no one will be surprised when it comes out.

-

Joe stands as soon as he sees me, and it's lucky he does because this restaurant is full—so much for Quinn's theory on people not eating dinner this early.

I'm excited for these two to meet, and I wonder if this is how Quinn felt the night Aleks came over. I'd be lying if I said Joe's approval wasn't important because I can already feel something deep here, and having my best friend and boyfriend not on the same page won't make things easy.

We reach the table where Joe's sat back down, and when his gaze slides from me to Quinn—Quinn tenses up beside me.

"So this is the boyfriend?" Joe asks.

"Yup. Quinnie, meet Joe."

There's a beat of silence between them. Awkward glancing away and back again, but I chalk it up to nerves.

"N-nice to meet you," Quinn rushes out, extending his hand and almost unending the table when his knee hits it.

"Whoa." I steady him, and he's blushing all the way to his ears.

"You too," Joe says, smothering his amusement.

They shake hands, and Quinn drops into his seat like he wants the thing to swallow him whole.

I send Joe an apologetic look. While I've seen Quinn like this, I never thought I'd have to give Joe the heads-up because he's hardly ever an awkward mess around me anymore.

"Are you okay?" I lean in and whisper.

"Yes, totally fine. Everything's fine." Quinn gives me a weak laugh before turning back to my friend. "So, *Joe*. Nice to meet you."

"You already said that," I point out.

"Right. I did. Yes."

I'm about to laugh over how adorable he is when it hits me. Quinn was like this around me when he found me attractive. Does *Joe* make him *that kind* of nervous?

Jesus fucking Christ, is he attracted to my *best friend*?

Kill me now.

I slump back in my chair, not exactly thrilled by the thought.

"You play for Buffalo, don't you?" Joe asks, and for right now, I hate his politeness.

"Sure do. It's great. Really great. It's how I met Vance—*professionally*. It was all professional. Nothing creepy or awkward or inappropriate." Quinn lets out that same weird laugh. "Okay, that makes it sound like I'm lying, but I'm definitely not. He didn't take advantage of me or anything. I—"

My eyes feel like they're ready to shoot from my skull as I pour a glass of water for him and nudge it his way. "Maybe you need a second?"

"Or ten," he says, physically deflating.

I turn to Joe, who's watching Quinn with amusement. Probably the exact same soft face I give him when he's being all adorable.

"He gets nervous easily," I explain.

"Wouldn't have guessed that. Hotshot hockey players usually have a reputation for overconfidence, don't they?"

"Unfortunately, I think the overconfident minority are just the ones that get the most attention."

"Like Ezra and Oskar and their sexcapades," Quinn says. He still doesn't sound normal, but at least he got a sentence out.

"Exactly." I wrap my hand around Quinn's, hating that I need to remind myself that he's mine. "My guy's more bashful than that."

"I can see that." Joe turns to his menu. "What should we order?"

That question distracts us for all of a minute, but the weirdness settles in again. Joe's trying to be chatty, but I'm distracted, and Quinn almost looks like he's trying to see how low he can sit before he disappears under the table.

"I'll admit I don't follow hockey much," Joe says. "How is Buffalo going this season?"

"Good," I answer. "They should make"—I redirect before Quinn can freak out over jinxing him again—"it high on the scoreboard. Quinn's had some amazing games lately."

"Lately?"

"I was injured!" Quinn all but shouts. "My adductor was strained, and then I tore it, but I did my rehab, and it's fine. Everything's great."

His gaze hasn't left his plate, and when Joe throws him a worried look, I know I can't get through the rest of dinner like this. But how do I bring up to my boyfriend that I know he thinks my friend is cute, but *dear God*, can he stop being so obvious about it?

"Quinn," I say, turning to him and trying to cut Joe out of the conversation. "Do you need a minute?"

"What? No. I'm fine."

I pin him with a look. "Don't bullshit me. What's going on?"

He sighs, golden eyes flicking to Joe and away again before he squeezes them tight. His answer is the absolute last thing I'm expecting. "I cheated on you."

My mouth drops, and as I'm struggling to find the words, I hear Joe mutter, "Oh, sweet Lord."

"You … *what*?"

"I'm sorry," he blurts, glancing over at Joe again.

And as the two of them lock eyes, pain slices through my chest. This swirling, sickly feeling fills my gut as a million thoughts fill my mind—Quinn's dry spell, Joe's family, what this means for us—but I can't take a second to process any of it because Quinn's still talking.

"I know him as Joel, and when I strained my adductor, it was *you* every time I walked into the training room. Even when I asked for Boone or O'Hennessy, you'd walk out all tight shirts and sexy smiles and being all 'you ready, Quinn?' and I don't know if you know this, but when you say my name …" He pretends to drool as I struggle to work out what he's saying. "Then the boner sitch would pop up, every fucking time, and you were so professional about it and all I could picture was your hands moving higher and it made me so embarrassed and I couldn't even say a single word to you—"

"Saying a lot of them now though." Joe sniggers.

I throw him a glare to shut the fuck up.

"You *cheated* on me," I repeat.

Quinn's face falls. "I started seeing Joe. On the sly. No one knew, not even management."

"Management?"

"I didn't even tell Boone."

"Why would you …" Some of my anger fades as the pieces click into place.

"I'm sorry," he tries again. "I thought if I kept telling you everything was fine, you wouldn't work on me, but I'd still be getting the help I needed and looking after myself."

"Wait." I choke on a relieved laugh. "You were seeing Joe … for *physiotherapy*?"

Quinn's brow wrinkles with confusion. "That's what I just said."

Relief crashes into me, and I drop my head into my hands. "Fucking hell."

"What's wrong?"

"You said you *cheated* on me. With Joe."

Awareness hits him. "Well, not like *that*."

Joe has to wipe tears from his eyes he's laughing so hard.

"Hilarious," I deadpan, but the effect is ruined by my smile. I lift Quinn's hand to my lips and press a kiss to the back of it. "You know I love the rambling and would never want you to change. But word choice is definitely something we're going to be working on in the future."

He gives me a sheepish look. "Is 'oops' an appropriate one right now?"

"Yep." I signal to the server. "And so is alcohol. We all need a drink after that."

CHAPTER TWENTY-FIVE

QUINN

Vance and Joel are still laughing at me. I don't think they've stopped, even while they were eating. I was worried they might choke. At first. Then I was hoping for it.

"I wish I could've been there," Vance says. "Quinn sneaking in, using a fake name—"

"Hey, I used my real last name. I just figured Asher was more incognito than Ayri."

Vance laughs again and wraps his arm around me. "No, it's adorable. Really, it is. I wish you could've told me or at least Boone why you were struggling, but I understand why you felt like you couldn't."

"And now I get to tease Vance over here about having my hands all over—"

Vance glares at Joel. "Don't even go there." The growl in his voice is super hot.

Vance's best friend laughs. "As much as I'd love to sit here and watch more of this, the kids should be asleep, so I'm going to go home to my wife and put my hands all over her."

"Good plan," Vance says.

"It was lovely to, uh, meet you in a social setting, Quinn." He shakes my hand as he stands from the table and then turns to Vance. "Vancelicious. Always fun seeing you."

Now it's my turn to laugh. "Vancelicious? Like bootylicious, but with one hundred percent more Vance?"

Joel squeezes my shoulder. "That was just for you. Some ammunition for payback."

"Thanks, Joel."

"Call me Joe. All my friends do. Joel is too professional for me."

I can't say the acceptance doesn't feel good. "Joe."

We watch him leave, but when I turn back to Vance, he's not staring after his friend. He's smiling at me.

"You're adorable, you know that?"

"Ugh. Adorable. My mustache is doing its job of making me look more rugged and manly, I see."

"Why is facial hair a sign of masculinity? And actually, why is the word 'adorable' inherently feminine?" He's got me there.

"Learned language behaviors over generations of words and their meanings?"

"Do you want to get into a philosophical discussion over dessert, or do you want to head home?"

I lean closer to him and rumble, "The only dessert I want is at home."

Vance's hand flies up to get a waiter's attention and ask for the check.

The more I'm with him, the more I see how much he's into me. At first, I think the doubt was coming from the fact Vance hadn't shown any interest at all until he knew I was into him, which, as everyone has pointed out, was fucking obvious. But now, being introduced to his friend, him hanging out with Aleks and Bilson, the constant sleepovers when we're not on the road, and just how easy it is between us when we are together, it's easy to see how he feels about me. I can sense it, like if I were to reach out, I could touch it.

We haven't been together long, but I'm already picturing visions of our future. Moving in together. Maybe adopting some animals from the shelter we volunteered at recently.

I'm trying not to get ahead of myself, but as we leave the restaurant, Vance practically dragging me through the parking lot to my car, I realize there's no more danger of falling for him. I've already gone and done it. My attraction to him before was strong, and it's only grown ever since he kissed me by the Queensboro Bridge. It could become a bodybuilder with how strong it is. A WWE fighter. A—

"What are you thinking about?" Vance asks when we reach my car.

"WWE."

He frowns. "Random, but okay. You all good?"

I step toward him, gripping his jacket and pulling him close. "I could be better."

"Yeah?"

"We could be naked. Playing naked games with each other."

"Like chess?"

I inch my lips closer to his. "More fun than chess."

"Ah, Jenga."

I chuckle. "You want me to say it, don't you?"

"I love when filthy words come out of your sweet mouth."

Jesus. I'm getting so worked up I don't even know if I'll make it home. "I want to fuck your face. Or your ass. One or the other. No, maybe both."

"I'm up for it. What else do you want to do to me?"

"Get you home, first of all. That would help. Get out of this cold."

Vance whines. "I thought you were going to say more dirty things to me."

"I will. At home. Where I'm not going to get so horny that I crash the car or come in my pants."

Vance hums. "Fine. A car crash would be bad."

"But not coming in my pants?"

"Nope. That … actually might be hot, but only if you can't get changed for hours afterward, and you're walking around all uncomfortable and wet, smelling like sex, and—"

"That sounds like my worst nightmare, actually."

Vance laughs. "Of course it does. Sometimes this naïve innocent streak comes out in you, and then other times, you're offering your body to me on a silver platter."

"I'm a very complicated man. Now, get in the car before my dick freezes off, and we won't be able to use it at all anymore."

"Can't have that."

I wish the snow wasn't hanging around because getting back to my place is long and slow. As much as I'd joke that dying for a BJ from Vance would be worth it, actually dying isn't on my schedule.

The speed, or should I say lack thereof, might kill us before we get there though. Cause of death: old age.

"We should've met Joe closer to one of our houses," Vance says.

"I can't agree more, and if I wasn't so adamant on getting us home safely, I might've asked you to take matters into your own hands before my dick tries to escape and drive the car for us."

"I'd pay to see that."

I shift in my seat. "I'd pay not to be so fucking hard."

"At least I'm not the only one getting frustrated by the traffic."

"I hate snow. Why do we live somewhere where there's snow?"

"We should move. The commute might be a bitch though."

And even though we're only joking around about this stuff, just him saying we should move makes me warm and fuzzy inside.

What doesn't make me warm and fuzzy is how long it takes to get home. It's so long that I don't think either of us is hard anymore, and that urgent need has simmered to a medium want. I want him—I don't think there will ever be a time where I won't want him—but the mood has passed.

"Want a drink or anything?" I ask after opening my door and letting him in.

"I'm still waiting on my dessert."

I lift my gaze to where Vance's eyes burn into me, and bam, in an instant, that lust, that passion, comes shooting back through me again.

When it came to having sex with my high school boyfriend, because we were each other's firsts, we did a lot of exploring, experimenting with different things, but when I moved to Buffalo to play for the farm team, it's not exactly like I missed the sex with him. It was never fire and sparks between us. It was ... nice. I think that's why I never went out and did the hookup thing since. Because while I enjoyed the sex, it wasn't how Ezra and Oskar shamelessly talk about it. It was never wild. It was never so hot that I'd want to do it all the time.

With Vance, all he has to do is look at me, and I'm ready to go. I haven't worked out if it's a deeper connection or if we're more right for each other or what. Maybe when I was closeted, I never fully embraced the gay sex thing.

Whatever it is, I can undoubtedly say no one and nothing has ever turned me on the way Vance does. "Straight to the bedroom?"

Vance takes off his coat, and I do the same, just in time for him to close in on me. "Too far."

We keep backing up until I'm pressed against the wall. "Sex in the foyer, then?"

He leans in and smells like his cologne—the same woodsy scent he wears at work—which only makes me harder. He lowers his head, bringing his lips to my ear. "I think I recall something about fucking my face?"

I groan. "I really, really want that."

"Only if I get to fuck yours right afterward."

The thought of Vance filling my mouth, of pushing so far back into my throat that my eyes water ... Damn, I want it. Need it.

"Vance ..." I whine.

"Mmhmm?"

The bastard wants me to say all the words. I'll be Mr. Chatty if it'll make him get on his knees for me.

I reach back and pull off my sweater and shirt and then go for my pants and pop the top button next. "You going to take care of this for me?" I reach inside my boxers and pull out my cock, stroking softly while parting my lips as a little sound of want falls from my mouth.

Vance lowers his head, staring between our bodies.

"I want you on your knees," I say, my voice taking on that raspy tone that makes me sound bossy.

Vance is so much bigger than me. He's put together. He's ... for lack of a better word, a proper grown-up. So watching as he wordlessly sinks to his knees, offering his mouth *to me*, it feels like so much more than sex. More than a BJ.

I run my hand through his hair while he pulls down my pants and underwear. Where there'd usually be some teasing—Vance likes to draw things out—there's nothing but determination as he engulfs me.

His warm, wet mouth goes from zero to sixty in a heartbeat. He bobs his head and sucks me deep, and I let him take control, but that's not what he wants. His hands glide up the back of my thighs and grip my ass, pulling my hips away from the wall.

The way he looks up at me, encouraging me to take this, to take his mouth and fuck his face like I promised him, it almost has me spilling over already, but I somehow manage to hold it back.

I try a few experimental thrusts, going deeper each time, but Vance doesn't even flinch. He takes everything I give him until I'm moving in and out of his mouth with such force I worry about his airways. Not enough to stop, but still, the thought is there.

Watching my cock disappear between his lips over and over again, the concentration line in his forehead, his gorgeous eyes blinking up at me and getting watery … it's the sexiest fucking thing I've ever seen.

Ever.

Including porn. And considering I've been single for two years, I've watched a lot of porn.

My breathing becomes stilted, hard to get enough air, but I'm not going to stop. I moan, teetering on the edge, and right before I fall, just as my orgasm begins to erupt, Vance moves a hand from my ass to between my legs, squeezing my balls. My whole body tenses, every muscle tightening as I fill his mouth.

He swallows it all, breathing through his nose until I finally stop convulsing. I've barely caught my breath by the time Vance stands and undoes his pants. "That was so fucking hot I'm only going to need your mouth for about a minute."

"That's good because I'm impatient. I want to drink you down. Taste every drop." My voice is laced with rasp and sounds like sex.

What I'm saying isn't even that dirty or scandalous, but I think because I was that blushing, bumbling idiot for so long, he sees me as this inexperienced or shy person.

I can be that guy. But not here.

Not during sex.

I don't pull up my pants, just keep them around my ankles. It only adds to the sense of rush, of that frantic need for a quickie, and it sends a thrill through me.

With me on my knees, ready for the face fucking of a lifetime, I start off slow like he did, but he's not having it.

Vance grips either side of my face and fucks me so hard, so fast. I'm able to take it, but it's not the cleanest way to have a blowjob. Saliva goes everywhere, dribbling out the side of my mouth. My eyes water, and my nose runs, but I can fucking take it.

His thrusts are short but frequent, his breathing just as rapid as his hips.

Slurps fill the room, long and loud.

He's frantic now, getting closer and closer, and then he whispers, "My hole."

I hum around him like a question. "Hmm?"

"I need your finger inside me. Fuck, touch me, and I'll explode."

He's not fucking wrong either. I get as far as playing with his rim, trying to tease him open, but before I can push through that tight ring of muscle, he lets go, and his load tries to choke me.

I swallow fast, but not fast enough. Cum joins the spit falling from my mouth. It's messy, it's dirty, and holy fucking hell is it sexy.

When he leans down to pull me up, I use my strength to bring him down to the floor instead.

We lie there on the hardwood floor, breathing heavily, staring at the crown molding on the ceiling of my foyer, and I don't know about him, but I can't wipe the smile from my face.

"Best dessert ever," he says.

"Agreed."

CHAPTER TWENTY-SIX

VANCE

Quinn:
Vancelicious …

Me:
No.

Quinn:
Would you prefer commando? I can't work
out which is more embarrassing.

Me:
We've got too many nicknames. I'll let you
choose one to commit to.

Quinn:
Gotta go with Vancelicious.

I laugh and lock my phone, knowing he has to be getting ready for his game against Boston soon. Before he left, I reminded him it's only three days, but I'd been saying that for both of our benefits. I'm usually on the away games, but since this is a relatively short one, O'Hennessy went this time. I told Boone I can cover *all* the away trips for the rest of the season, but he said I can't expect him to rearrange the already set schedule for my sex life. Guess he saw right through that one.

Time apart is supposed to be a good thing in relationships, right?

I'm just not used to *missing* someone. Because I miss him a thousand percent more than I thought I would.

Him stretching in my living room, using my weights, stumbling around in my kitchen making his morning protein shake. I miss pressing a kiss to his hair as I turn the coffee machine on and cooking double portions for dinner. I'm a stupid lovesick idiot, but even when he's here with me, I want more.

His scent is all over my sheets, so I wash them to spare myself the torture and immediately regret it. This

228

relationship stuff is *hard*. How can I be so obsessively happy and pining at the same time?

Quinn joked about me becoming his sex master, and I can't say I'm all that opposed to the idea right now.

Instead of spending my time obsessing over him, I pull on some layers and go for a walk around the city. This is why it's important to have other interests outside of hockey, and it's something I worry Quinn is still missing. When things overwhelm me, I just leave the house and *go*. It sounds like such a low-key pointless hobby, but I like to look at things. Interesting things. I'm no architect, but fancy buildings, light posts, those telephone boxes they have in England … I just *like* them. Bridges are my favorite, and I enjoyed sharing it with Quinn, even though he doesn't get it. He doesn't have to.

I've seen almost everything there is to see in Buffalo at this point, and I've covered a lot of ground in the cities we've visited. When I retire, I want to go all over Europe. Having that goal for the future is something that stops me from getting too bogged down in the here and now.

I wish I could give that to Quinn. An escape from current pressures. I want to solve all of his problems for him and keep him safe, but while he might be sweet and naïve at times, he's a smart man who can figure things out for himself. All he needs is a little nudge, and I've already given him that. I have to trust he can work things out for himself.

The walk doesn't last nearly long enough, so when I get home, I clean and call my mom and then work through a list of menial tasks to take up time until his game. What the hell did I do with my time *before* I started seeing him?

Nothing I want to be doing now.

It's a relief when the game against Boston gets started. I sit down with my beer, prepared to watch the whole thing, exactly like I would if I was there live. Only this time. I'll be getting pissed at the producers for not focusing the footage on Quinn the entire game.

When the team skates out, my focus immediately zeros in on him and his movements. It's habit by this point, but now we're together, there's also this obsessive need growing to make sure he's in top shape. I know how his mind works, and I know how easy it is for one tiny twinge to fuck him up mentally, but from what I can tell, he looks good.

Fingers crossed for another great game.

Ten minutes in and I can already tell it isn't going to be a good game. Quinn isn't fucking up on anything, but Boston is wiping the floor with the whole team. It looks like last year's Buffalo is showing up to play, and while Quinn, Dalton, and Müller all get some good plays in, there's only so much Chenkin can do against the bullets Anton Hayes is firing his way. Hayes and Palaszczuk aren't as openly affectionate as the Mitchell brothers—I cringe at the habit of that nickname, considering they're actually husbands—but the fist bumps and occasional ass slap by Palaszczuk speak volumes. Two men in a public relationship, dominating at the highest level of the game.

And they're playing against another two openly queer men.

Which … Buffalo might not be at their best tonight, but just seeing all those guys out there, living as their most authentic selves, it makes me a little teary.

It's not something I ever saw or dreamed of seeing growing up, and I can only imagine the impact those four men are having on young hockey kids today.

And I get to call Ayri Quinn all mine.

As soon as the game wraps up seven to two, Boston's way, I fire off a string of texts telling Quinn not to be too hard on himself, and I'm proud of how he played and that he can call if he needs to.

The hardest part is the wait afterward. I know he'll be cooling down, showering, maybe dealing with reporters. He's not called out for the press conference, thank fuck, but Dalton is hauled up there like they want to show off his PR training. And I'll give it to him, when someone asks about West, instead of his stock response, he just gives them a dirty look and asks for the next question.

It's not until an hour later that I finally get a text.

Quinn:
Wish you didn't see that.

Me:
Why? It wasn't your best game, but you weren't back in that bad headspace. You guys got unlucky.

Quinn:
I let you down.

Me:
Impossible. Don't say stupid things.

Quinn:
I don't want to go out.

Me:
So don't?

Quinn:
Collective rules.

Me:
Fuck the rules.

Quinn:
Did you miss the part about Ezra being Ezra-ish? Besides, if I leave Dalton with those two solo, it won't end well.

Me:

Then at least try to enjoy yourself.

Quinn:

Not gonna happen. Sorry, Vance. I really
wanted to take home the W for you.

I immediately try to call him to set him straight, but he doesn't answer his phone. He doesn't reply when I tell him all that "for me" stuff was bullshit. I just wanted Quinn to stop focusing internally so much out there. He needs to be playing for him. For his team.

I'm kicking myself for not grabbing Dalton's number when I had the chance, but there's literally no reason for me to have it. I'm not going to text him to report back that Quinn's okay. And it's not like I can just reach out to Ezra fucking Palaszczuk through social media and hope that he replies.

I rake both hands back through my hair, frustrated with myself that I didn't just call Quinn to begin with. I hate that he's being hard on himself, and I hate even more that he thinks he's let me down. The only thing letting me down is not being there with him, to make sure he knows that one game—that wasn't even all that bad—doesn't matter in the scheme of things. Sure, he's only just gotten back on his line, but he's still there. Coach wouldn't pull him when the rest of the team played equally as mediocre.

He's sulking, and I have to hope he's okay. Trust him to pull through this and not let it affect his next game.

At 2:00 a.m., my ringtone blaring in the dark wakes me up.

I scramble for it, gut in my throat at the thought that something happened, and find a video call from Quinn.

I give my eyes a quick scrub so I don't look half-asleep, try to control my smile, and answer.

"Bit later than I was expecting you," I say huskily, angling the phone so a good part of my chest is on display.

But instead of Quinn's face—or even better, naked body—the screen is filled with a mouth so close to the camera I can't make out much else. And those pouty lips definitely aren't Quinn's.

"Vance …" the mouth slurs. "Sexy, sexy Vance …"

"Hello?"

"Stop hogging the pretty shirtless man," another voice says, and when the phone is jostled, I get a quick flash of Hayes and Palaszczuk.

"Where's Quinn?" I ask, but it's useless because those two are bickering between themselves. When the phone stops shaking like it's at a rave, Ezra Palaszczuk is back.

"What are your insentions with fairy?"

Oh dear God. "Insentions?"

Hayes sniggers. "Inseminations?"

"Insurections," Palaszczuk adds.

"What the hell are you two talking about?" comes Dalton's voice from off-screen, and when the phone shakes again, I assume he's gone for it, but Ezra's mouth reappears.

"Little D almost touched me to get the phone back. He really loves you. He lurrrves you."

"It's *Quinnie's* boyfriend," Hayes says. "Not Little D's."

"Little D." Palaszczuk chuckles.

But I'm still stuck on that boyfriend thing. Sure, that's what we've talked about being, but it's the first time I've been called that by someone, and it feels ridiculously good.

"Is there a point to this call?" I ask lower this time, and it finally gets their attention.

"Yes. Insen … Inten …"

"Intentions?"

Palaszczuk gives a throaty laugh. "Yes. What are they?"

"Whatever he wants them to be. Ideally, to look after him and make him happy."

And if I thought that was going to score me points with his friends, I clearly don't know them at all.

Palaszczuk makes a buzzer sound while Hayes shakes his head.

"Wrong," Hayes groans.

"So, so wrong. The only asseptible answer is give him a good fuckening. Deep dive with your dick. Make Quinnie singy."

Apparently, drunk hockey players are idiots. Who knew? "Sure," I deadpan. "All that too."

Palaszczuk pretends to muffle a sob as he swipes a tear from his eye. Then the phone goes blurry again as he moves—

And apparently climbs on the table. "I heretoforefather bless this … sanction?"

"Union," Anton calls.

"Reunion of boy parts and slutty hearts. And when—"

"Hey! What the hell are you doing with my phone, asshole?"

I sag with relief at Quinn's—sober-sounding—voice.

Palaszczuk obviously doesn't fight Quinn for his phone because a moment later, his beautiful face appears. Unsurprisingly, a blush covers his cheeks.

"I'm so sorry. I went to take a piss and came back to this dickhead table dancing with my boyfriend's head."

"Mmm, head …" one of the drunk ones says from off-screen.

"*Stop.*"

A round of laughter follows Quinn's shout.

"Yeah, that was an, uh, interesting way to wake up."

"I'm sorry."

"Don't be," I say, stifling a yawn. "I want to meet your other friends. Just maybe not at 2:00 a.m. when I'm expecting phone sex and they're so drunk they don't know which way is up."

"That might be my fault."

"*Might* be?"

"I bet them they couldn't do a shot for every goal they scored tonight, and then Asher bet Palaszczuk couldn't drink them faster than Hayes."

"Now, I could be wrong, but you almost sound like … you're enjoying yourself."

He tries to catch his smile, but it slips through. "Considering Ezra and Anton are always fucking with the

236

rest of us, it's nice to get them back for a change. Though Anton's surprisingly good at holding his alcohol and isn't anywhere near as embarrassing as Ezra is."

"Bet him that he can't hat trick double shots. That should do it."

"Ooh, good idea."

"I'll let you get back to your friends."

Uncertainty crosses his face. "You don't *have* to."

"Sure, I do. It's purely selfish. I like knowing you're having fun."

He narrows his eyes. "You just wanna go back to sleep."

"Oh, damn, you caught me." While I might be tired, I was serious about the fun thing. "Do your friends play tomorrow?"

"Nope. They have two days off, so I have zero guilt over getting them wasted."

"Even when you're being mean, you're still a total sweetheart."

"Vance …" he pretends to whine. "Not in front of the guys."

I laugh at how big and tough Quinn tries to be. Speaking of … "You didn't let me down."

"What?"

"Your message earlier. I don't want you to ever worry about that. You're allowed to feel shitty about hockey or how you played, but never, ever about me. Got it?"

Quinn bites his lip, eyes bright. "Got it."

"Good." I press a big kiss to the camera. "Bye, babe."

His whole face softens, and he whispers, "Miss you."

Fuck. I've never spoken words I mean more when I answer, "Miss you too."

CHAPTER TWENTY-SEVEN

QUINN

Other than that one little blip against Boston, my playing has stayed strong. It took a bit of convincing and sports psychology from Vance, but once I was able to get out of my head on my own, without tricking it into thinking I was playing well for him, my hot streak continued.

After possibly the worst beginning to a season for me personally, I'm racking up points and have helped carry the team to where we are now. Game one, series one, of the goddamn Stanley Cup playoffs.

I might not have broken any records like Asher to get here, but we're fucking *here*. And if Asher doesn't take out the Calder Trophy for rookie of the year, I'll eat my hat. Though not literally, because there's a good chance his reputation for being less than friendly might make the writers' association give it to someone else to prove a point.

Hockey isn't just about the game. It's about image. It's about teamwork. And while Asher has that down pat on the ice, off it, he's a hot mess.

With how the bracket falls this season, we're playing Boston first up, and I don't want a repeat of the last time we faced off with them.

Vance is off for the next two games because he'll be coming with us to Boston for games three and four, so I would have been the last of the team to arrive at the arena if it weren't for Vance practically kicking me out because, in his words, my mind should be on hockey not on sex. Even the argument that getting out of my head has helped me with my games didn't work this time.

And to be fair, if I had stayed, we would've ended up naked, and I would've been late.

So instead, I'm horny and one of the first to arrive at our home arena. Asher's the only one who's beaten me here. He's already at his cubby, base layers on, AirPods in, trying to get in the zone.

I join him, and he takes one of his pods out.

"We're going to kick their asses," I say.

"We have to. It's Ezra."

I laugh. "Did you see Seattle and Vegas are pitted against each other in series one of their conference? If the brackets weren't based on stats from the regular season, I'd suspect the NHL was purposefully making teams with queer players take out other queer players."

"Considering no one from the Collective even made it to the playoffs last season, we're sure as fuck making up for it this time."

"Poor Oskar and Foster. The only two who didn't make it."

Asher's lips twitch.

"You're going to be all gloaty about that, aren't you?"

He gasps. "Me? Never. You don't kick a man when he's down."

"Unless that man is Ezra?"

"Precisely."

We joke, but this is a big deal. My knee bounces with nerves. This could be the first game of the rest of our lives. Or whatever that phrase is.

The Buffalo franchise hasn't made the playoffs in over a decade, but this season, everything has just worked. Well, for everyone else except for me, but I've picked up my game, and this is my chance to prove to everyone that injured and unsure Quinn is gone. I'm future first-line material. Future Hall of Famer. And if I keep telling myself that, maybe I'll actually achieve it one day.

Asher nudges me. "We've got this."

"Do we?"

"Yep. And even if we don't, we've taken the team further than they've been in years."

"Sure. It was all us too."

"All me, maybe." Asher grins.

I'm not even going to call him out for being a cocky son of a bitch because when he's like this, he's unstoppable on the ice, and we need that.

He doesn't seem to be feeling the pressure at all, and maybe it's because it's only game one—we'll have six more chances to win this series. Or maybe he is, and that's why he has his confident façade in place.

Okay, time to block out the pressure of needing to do well. It's game one of a possible seven. If we fuck up, it's not the end of the world. Yet.

And while it would be amazing for team morale if we went out there and smashed the competition to pieces, we don't have to.

It's just another night on the ice.

Just another game.

No need to crack under the pressure because there is no pressure.

I throw my head back. "Fuck, this isn't working."

"What's not?"

"All I can concentrate on is that we need to win. No matter how many times I tell myself this game is important but not as important as games four, five, six, and seven."

"We're not taking this series to seven. I won't let it. And neither will you. Here." He hands over one of his AirPods. "Listen to music to drown out that annoying voice."

"Yours, you mean?"

"Throw all the insults you want, Quinnie. Whatever distracts you."

"It's not fun if you welcome it," I grumble.

It's what I need. It's changing my mindset. I close my eyes and listen to the rock mix he's listening to, bopping my head in time with the beat and doing nothing but relaxing and focusing on only the music.

When it's time to dress for the game and in that small window between warm-ups and the puck drop, I'm as ready as I think I'll ever be.

Asher and I chest bump, and he slaps the back of my helmet before we head down the chute. "We're not taking this to game seven." He's so determined, so sure, that it's easy to believe him.

"No game seven."

—

We took it to fucking game seven.

The first night, we killed it, and it was the best start to a playoffs series in history. Okay, that might be exaggerating, but we wiped the floor with them. Second game was the same deal. Then, out of fucking nowhere or the sheer pressure of losing to us, Ezra and Anton upped their game and scraped in a W. Then we took out the next. We were sure we had it in the bag, but we fell apart under the pressure.

And that's how we got here. Game seven. Third period all wrapped up, and we're sitting at three apiece.

This bitch is going into overtime.

There's only one goal in it.

Asher and I aren't on first shift, and the play goes back and forth so fast it's like we're watching tennis, not hockey.

My knee starts bouncing again, and Asher puts a gloved hand on my leg to stop me.

Vance is on tonight, and in the next moment, he's leaning over from his spot behind the team, his lips in my ear. "When you're out there, just focus on me. Believe in me, not in you."

I nod. "Don't believe in myself. Got it."

243

Vance's warm chuckle sends a shiver down my spine. "Exactly."

"That's some fucked-up logic," Asher cuts in, but he doesn't get it.

If in doubt, whenever that voice tries to tell me I'm not good enough or I'll fuck it up, I think of how Vance sees me. How much faith he has in me. I can trust him. I can't trust my own opinion of myself.

Coach sends us out there, neither team even coming close to scoring yet, and knowing Buffalo's third line is out here, Boston sends out their first, and it's Asher against Anton.

With Ezra blocking our fucking path to victory.

Vance, Vance, Vance. Believe in the Ayri Quinn Vance believes in.

Asher manages to pry the puck away from Anton hogging the damn thing, and he somehow manages to get on a breakaway. I fly down the ice on his right and see Ezra heading for Asher from in front of me. It's like I can see the disaster coming before it happens, and I'm in the perfect position to intervene. Instead of going around the back of him and trying to score, I protect my center by skating in front of Ezra. There's a risk of getting a penalty for tripping, but if I get there in time … He collides into me, which I knew he would, and we both go crashing to the ice.

The best part? Instead of a tripping penalty, he gets a penalty for charging.

I just got us the power play of our fucking lives.

Which Asher and I follow up with the goal of our fucking lives. He's been shooting bullets all season, so Boston's goalie covers him and forgets about little ol' me waiting goal side for Asher to pass at the last second. Before Griffith has a chance to turn—he's fast, but not that fucking fast—my shot goes sailing right by him.

The relief is immediate, the weight lifting off my shoulders in an instant.

We celebrate like crazy on the ice.

One series down. Three more to go.

At the handshake after the game, Ezra squeezes my hand just a little too tight. "I don't know whether to be mad at you or proud of you."

Anton shoves him from behind and takes my hand. "He's proud of you. Great game." Then he leans in. "Since you knocked us out, you better bring home more rings for the Collective."

The team is on an absolute high as we walk down the chute and into the locker room. The air is buzzing, and the energy is just so fucking amazing that I don't even think before marching right up to Vance and wrapping my arms around him for a hug.

Probably not appropriate, but he takes it even further than that. When I pull back, he cups my cheek and kisses the fuck out of me in front of the team, Coach, everyone. It's short but hot.

"You played fucking amazing," he murmurs when he pulls away.

"I knew it!" Müller calls out.

"Pfft. We all did," Chenkin says. "Quinn's been walking around with a permanent smile on his face, and he's always looking at Vance with cartoon love-heart eyes."

I don't even care about the teasing. "I don't think we were very subtle," I say to Vance.

"That goal was anything but subtle."

"Quinn, Dalton. Press conference," our PR manager says.

We quickly change into team sweats and T-shirts and go do the PR thing, boasting about teamwork and how amazing it is to get the winning goal for the series.

It's the first time in a press conference Asher doesn't get asked about his retired brother, so we're both walking on air when we get back to the locker room.

"No wonder you've been so happy lately," Ducre says. "I thought it was because you got your spot on your line back."

"Nah, it's the honeymoon period," Müller says.

Jost, one of our defensemen, adds, "Just wait until that's over. Then it's all relationship obligations that feel like a ball and chain. There's a reason marriage is nicknamed that."

My good mood sobers, and I stare at the treatment room, where Vance is already working on someone's shoulder and can't hear what's going on out here.

It's not like Vance and I are going to get married or anything. What we have at the moment is amazing. But … is it just a honeymoon phase? What I have with him I never had with my ex, so it's almost like I'm going into this

246

blind to what a grown-up relationship looks like. What if he gets sick of me just like my ex did?

If this is just the honeymoon phase, when does the fighting kick in?

-

No matter how hard I try to pick a fight with Vance, he doesn't take the bait. I'm irrationally moody for the whole playoffs, nitpick every little thing he does, and do all the annoying habits I can think of to get him to have some kind of reaction—any reaction. But all he does is accept it and then look at me like, "Aww, poor baby, he's going through so much."

Dude, no. Just yell at me. Snap. Do *something*.

One good thing about me stressing over when that shoe will inevitably drop is I'm in that perfect headspace between focusing on hockey and being distracted enough that I don't think on the ice. I just do. Asher, Müller, and I get more ice time than ever before because there's something about the three of us that is clicking. It's how we wipe out Tampa in the semifinals in six games and earn ourselves a much-needed break before the finals.

Buffalo is in the fucking finals of the Stanley Cup Championships. A chance to take home the Cup for the first time in the franchise's history.

Shit, no pressure.

Müller throws a viewing party for game seven between Seattle and Colorado from the other side of the bracket. Whoever wins this game will be facing us for the Cup.

The entire team is here, but no one is drinking because we're all making sure we're at peak performance for these next seven games.

Vance is standing beside me, behind Müller's couch in his living room that's filled with hockey players sprawled out everywhere—the floor, recliners, couches—but I'm too nervous to sit. I'd rather be on my feet.

Vance is sipping beer, and for a split second, I contemplate yelling at him for doing something the rest of us can't do. It doesn't even annoy me, but fuck, not knowing what our first fight is going to be about is making me more anxious than it should. I guess in my mind, if I pick a fight over something small and we can get through that, then maybe I'll believe when the relationship goes to hell with constant fighting like some of the horror stories the team has told me about their wives that we can survive that too.

"Come on, Colorado," Chenkin says from right in front of the TV.

"Nah, we want to be playing Seattle," Ducre says, and I agree.

Not because Seattle has had a killer season but has struggled through the playoffs and look tired, but because if we can't win the Cup, I'd rather it go to another team with a queer player.

I bite my thumbnail and sway on my feet, waiting to see the result. It's a fucking nerve-racking game and so close. Every time one of them scores, the other team follows it up, but Colorado is in the lead by one, and the clock is ticking down.

Asher, on the other side of me, says, "I don't care who wins because it'll be just as much fun to kick Colorado's ass as it will Seattle's."

Everyone laughs, but I shake my head at him, and in the split second I'm not paying attention, Aleks evens the damn score.

Even though it might be bad karma, everyone jumps up and cheers when the game goes into overtime.

We'll be going into the final series refreshed and rested. Whoever we face will be exhausted. Any advantage, we're going to take.

No matter who we face.

But please let it be Seattle.

And thanks to a goal by Dennan Katz in overtime, it will be.

CHAPTER TWENTY-EIGHT

VANCE

The pressure of the playoffs is getting to Quinn. Not on the ice though. There, he's still dominating. Off the ice, when we're alone, he's … off. Stressed, probably, but I'd be lying if I said I wasn't missing my sweet, clueless, sometimes filthy man.

Stressed Quinn is not a fun Quinn, and while I can handle him having moments like this—everyone does—it's only been getting worse as the playoffs have gone on. We'll be having a perfectly normal dinner, and then it's like he remembers himself, and his scowl snaps back into place. If I didn't know better, I'd think he and Dalton body-swapped because Dalton is loving life. He's playing like he's been in the NHL for ten years, not a rookie, and he's constantly … happy. Like he thrives under pressure. Quinn could take some pointers from him.

Some days, he's still the sweet, innocent man I'm falling for. Others, I want to smother him with a pillow.

I switch off the TV and toss the remote on the bed, and one good thing about us being officially out as a couple means we share a room at away games.

"It doesn't go there," Quinn mutters, crossing the room to pick up the remote and move it to the nightstand. And while this side of him is getting a bit much, he's still so goddamn cute when he's grumbly. I'm just holding out hope that we get that Cup and Quinn can finally relax again.

There are only seven more games in it. Hopefully less though.

We're getting so close now that it's a hope even *I* won't voice out loud. I'm not used to being so high-strung, watching what I say, and being cautious not to do anything that will get in his head. I know how much of Quinn's game is mental, and I'd hate myself if I said the wrong thing, which resulted in him screwing up and losing them the Cup.

That's just not something Quinn would ever let go.

"You almost ready to head out?"

"I want to change my shirt."

"Really?" I eye the midnight-blue button-up he's wearing, loving the way it makes his golden eyes brighter. "I like it."

"Well, I don't."

Okay. I smother my reply with a deep breath and refuse to look any more into it than him not liking the damn shirt. We're going out for a quiet dinner with Aleks and his boyfriend, Gabe. I'm still not sure that meeting up with the opposition is a smart move—Dalton flipped the night off with both hands and mumbled something about not giving Aleks a chance to get in his head or ruin his good mood—but I don't even feel like mentioning that would be supportive for Quinn, who's about two seconds away from crumbling under the pressure.

How do WAGs deal with their man-child once a season?

With any luck, I'll get to find out. Other than this brief period, Quinn makes me happier than anyone I've ever met. It's easy to see a long future ahead with him, and while there's so much that can get in the way of that—a trade being a big one—I hope we get the chance to explore it. If only we can get through the next week or two.

He walks out of the bathroom in a shirt no different from the one he was wearing, and before I can stop myself, I grab his waist and pull him to me. Grumpy or not, I need a moment just to remind myself of the guy I'm falling for.

Thankfully, I've caught him at a good moment because he melts into my hug, arms clinging to the back of my coat.

"Ready to go?"

"I think so." He sighs.

"You've got your truce," I remind him. I might not think this dinner is a smart idea, but like hell I'm not going to be supportive. No hockey talk is the rule for tonight, and if I've gotta be the asshole to enforce that rule, I sure as hell will.

"Yeah, good."

"And when we come back, I'll give you a nice long massage until you're good and relaxed, then get you off so you sleep like the dead."

"You're kinda perfect," he says, but there's something cutting in his tone. Like being perfect isn't a good thing.

"No one's perfect, Ayri." And maybe I'm shorter with him than I want to be, but if he's having second thoughts about us, that's going to hurt.

"Yeah. Okay. You ready?"

"I'm ready."

He gives a curt nod, then takes my hand, and him reaching for me helps calm that brief flicker of doubt.

Aleks has booked out a private booth at the back of the restaurant, but when we walk past the full tables, I still notice a few looks thrown our way. I'm ready to interfere if anyone throws even a minor chirp his way and don't relax until we've made it through.

There are three men waiting, Aleks, Bilson, and Gabe, who I haven't met yet. He's the largest of the three, with a Superman-strong jawline and dimpled smile.

"Gabe," he says, reaching a large hand across the table.

"Vance. You're Aleks's partner?"

"Yup. And you're Quinn's."

Quinn huffs and pulls me into the seat next to him. "He's also a team trainer, and a bridge enthusiast, and a geocacher, and a pro-massager. He's not *just* my boyfriend."

Aleks laughs. "You sound like me when I was having a freak-out over Gabe."

"I'm not freaking out." Quinn scowls.

"He's stressed with work," I point out, setting a steady hand on Quinn's thigh. He rests his over the top.

"Something you know all about," Gabe throws at Aleks. "I swear I haven't seen him for weeks. He's either away or training."

"What happened to no hockey talk?" Aleks actually crosses his arms.

"Who said hockey? I didn't say hockey. Just commiserating with Vance over having to deal with the world ending if you don't beat the other team at putting a disc in a net."

"I'm going through it too," Bilson says. "And I don't have anyone to deal with my whining."

"Is that why you're here at a Collective meet-up again?" Quinn asks.

"No, he's hiding," Gabe says in a mocking voice and turns to Bilson. "Since you broke up with Rina, I've had to deal with the both of you."

"I'm not hiding from Rina!" Bilson gasps.

"Not *only* Rina. From half of Seattle." Aleks laughs. "Hey, at least you broke up with Gabe's work friend before marrying her. Progress!"

"Wait." I look between the three of them. "Why are you hiding from half the people in Seattle?"

"Because everywhere I go, I run into one of my ex-wives or girlfriends. I'm beginning to think it's a conspiracy theory."

"If you hadn't married every woman in Seattle, it wouldn't be an issue," Aleks points out.

Gabe snorts. "And why you thought you *wouldn't* run into Rina at the station when you picked me up is beyond me."

"She swapped shifts! How was I supposed to know?"

"Why don't you avoid going into the station?" Quinn asks.

And suddenly, Bilson's issues are making grumpy Quinn seem pleasant.

"Because Aleks always wants to go there. This is why it's a dumb idea to date someone you're always going to have to cross paths with." Bilson points at Gabe. "At least if anything ever happened with you and Aleks, you can avoid each other."

"Unless Ezra tries to set me on fire again," Quinn deadpans. But before I can ask what *that's* about, Gabe huffs and pulls Aleks to him.

"You shut your face when you're speaking to us." Gabe sends Bilson an intimidating glare.

Bilson spins on Quinn. "Got any room at Buffalo? I need to get out of this city before one of my exes kills me ... or Gabe does."

"Buffalo only has so many women," I say.

"You really need to get away that badly?" Quinn asks. "I couldn't imagine asking for a trade."

"Oh, trust me," Bilson says, gaze flicking toward me so briefly I almost miss it. "Relationship breakdowns are the worst. The tension. The anger. The petty bitterness. I just want it to stop."

"Maybe if you'd, I don't know, stop falling in love with every woman you sleep with, you wouldn't be in this position," Aleks says.

"But they're all so—*shit*." Bilson practically dives under the table.

"Well, that's normal." I turn to Quinn, expecting to find him grinning back, but he's just staring at Bilson's vacated seat.

"Naomi just walked in," Aleks says, craning to look around the partitions separating us from the rest of the restaurant.

"Who's Naomi?" Quinn asks.

"His first wife," Aleks says.

"Out of curiosity," I say, "how many have there been?"

"I want to say … three?"

"Four," comes the squeak from below us.

Four divorces? I can't even comprehend one, let alone *four*. "How does he still have a cent to his name?"

"Excellent lawyers."

Probably cheaper to keep a whole legal team on retainer than divorce four separate women with the money he earns.

I laugh. "Maybe you *should* sign with Buffalo."

Quinn stiffens beside me. "But who would we trade?" The tension in his voice makes me lean over and kiss his head.

"Not you after the playoffs you've had."

"Yeah. Maybe."

I squeeze his thigh, hoping that wordless support gets through to him better. There's zero possibility of Buffalo *wanting* to trade him, but you just never know. Playing at the top of his game can sometimes make for a very enticing bargaining chip, but there's no way Buffalo would ever trade him *and* Dalton. Those two working together are a powerhouse.

"Who does have room?" Aleks asks.

Gabe lifts his hands in surrender. "That is *not* a me question. Other than your friends' teams, I have no idea where the rest of them are."

I rub my jaw as I scroll through the teams. "Since Strömberg retired, New York still hasn't tightened up their forward line. I think Dallas and Tennessee both need some magic in that area too. Though Dallas also needs a solid D-man, and Tennessee's goalie keeps reinjuring himself."

"Yeah, but Tennessee has that backup goalie. The one who just got moved up from the farm team. He's filled in for a lot of games this year, and the guy's got talent," Aleks says. "I wouldn't be surprised if he's their starting goalie next season."

Bilson huffs, peeking out from under the table. "Miles Olsen? He's a cocky little shit in that fratty dude-bro kind of way."

Gabe pats Bilson's head. "Then it's settled. You can stay with Seattle."

"Yeah, you can't abandon me and Katz," Aleks says.

"Ooh, discord in Seattle," I taunt. "That bodes well for us."

"Nuh-uh." Gabe slaps a large hand on the table. "No psyching my man out. I might not get it, but we had a deal, and I understand those."

"Sorry, sorry, my bad."

Quinn's still being unusually quiet. I can't imagine how nervous he must be going into the championship, but I can feel it in my bones that they're going to be some of the best games I've ever seen him in.

Again, never saying that out loud. All I'm doing until it's over and done with is keeping my mouth shut and playing the role of good little boyfriend.

"Will you be on the Collective trip this off-season?" Gabe asks, startling me out of my thoughts.

"What do you mean?"

"Apparently, they try to catch up for a weeklong vacation. This will be my first one."

Quinn shifts. "I haven't been on one either. Skipped last year's."

But that's all he says. It's the first I'm hearing about it, and considering it sounds like he's going, I'm a bit hurt he didn't think to mention it. A whole week away? I'd never stop him, but considering I'm expecting most of my off-season plans to revolve around him, I'd have appreciated the heads-up that he's not going to be here.

And telling Gabe I'm not invited on their trip is awkward as fuck.

"That sounds awesome," I say, thankfully sounding normal. "I'm glad you all have that support network." I turn to smile at Quinn, and he's already studying my face. "I bet you'll have a great time."

"Yeah … probably."

The waiter comes around to take our orders, but I suddenly don't feel like eating anymore. Still, I choke the food down, reminding myself that the season is almost over.

CHAPTER TWENTY-NINE

QUINN

Vance is an idiot, but the more crap he takes from me, the more I'm realizing *I'm* the idiot. It started at the beginning of the playoffs, when my stupid teammates put the ridiculous idea in my head that we were on some kind of honeymoon phase and it will all blow up. So instead of shrugging it off and telling myself Vance and I will be different, I've dwelled on it. For almost a whole month.

All I can say I've learned from this experience is that Vance is a goddamn saint. And, possibly, I might be as superstitious as Ezra. Because the longer this tension has gone on, the longer I have nagged Vance over the little things, the better I've been playing.

So now I don't even want to stop, even though I know I'm getting over-the-top diva on him.

It's a messed-up cycle, but it's working. What if I break, tell Vance what's going on in my head, and then we lose the magic on the ice when we are so. Damn. Close? Yeah, I'm going to need to do some serious groveling once all of this is over.

The series is going amazingly well. We only need to win one more game. One more fucking game out of three.

But we don't have the home advantage for the next game. We won't have the home crowd, the familiar ice …

Just one more win.

"Babe." Vance shakes me from where I'm still half-asleep, trying to convince myself to get out of bed because today's the day. This is the night.

We're going to take out the Cup.

Yep.

Just end it now so I can stop being a dickhead to my boyfriend.

Damn it.

I roll over to face Vance and crack open my eyes. "What?"

"You're talking in your sleep. Saying 'one more win, one more win,' over and over again."

"Oh, I wasn't asleep. I'm trying to get myself to get out of bed."

Vance chuckles. "I wish I could do something to take the pressure off." His eyes widen, and he uncharacteristically starts rambling like I would when in an awkward situation. "Not that I'm saying you're cracking under the pressure or you're not playing well or anything like that, I just—"

"Wait …" I assess Vance's face and, maybe for the first time in a few weeks, notice the bags under his eyes. Then there are the worry creases in his forehead. "Are you worried I'm about to snap at you or something?"

"Well, aren't you? You've been borderline snippy ever since the playoffs started, and it's getting to the point I don't want to say anything for fear of setting you off in a sulky mood. The most annoying part is you don't even confront it—you just pick at every little thing I do. There's no way I can help if I don't know what's pissing you off."

I groan and cover my face with the pillow.

"I told myself I wasn't going to bring it up while you have to focus on hockey, but technically, you brought it up."

I grunt and don't remove the pillow so I can get this out. "I've been doing the same thing."

Vance pulls my pillow away. "How so?"

As I think about how I've been acting, how distant I've been, worried about when we may or may not fight because I know it's coming, and then not saying anything because we've been killing these playoffs, I realize the extent of my ridiculousness.

"Okay, so at first, right, you know, after the team found out? They said we both look happy and never stop smiling, and—"

He gasps. "Those assholes!"

"They are assholes, but they didn't mean to be. They said to enjoy the honeymoon period while I have the chance because it'll end, and then we'll fight. And then we went to dinner, and Bilson was hiding from his ex-wife, and when Asher was missing Kole, he was even more unbearable than ever before."

Vance takes a deep breath. "So you started freaking out about us fighting and pulled away a bit."

"Yup. Well, at first, I was trying to taunt you into little fights by getting snippy at you over stupid shit—"

"Like where the remote goes?"

"Exactly. And then ... then the team was doing so well in the playoffs it kinda became a routine. Like a superstition. I told myself I wouldn't bring it up, because what if we talked it out and then our game tanked?"

Vance tries to hold back his smile, but he fails epically. "Fuck, you hockey players are intense when it comes to superstition crap."

"I didn't think it was my thing, but this season it has been. Just the playoffs, actually. We're so close to winning I can taste it, and I'm terrified the team is just going to crumble under the pressure. I'm scared I'll crumble under it. Which is also why I didn't say anything. Having this tension between us has been good for my game because I'm not focused solely on hockey. You're always there in the back of my mind."

Vance cups my cheek. "Can't I be in the back of your mind with happy thoughts instead of tension because I gotta say, I hate, hate, hate the nitpicky side of you."

"So do I! And I'm sorry, so, so sorry for being short with you and not showing you love the way you deserve it. But once I started, it just kept going and going and going, and even when I knew I should stop, I was too scared to."

"Because of the hockey."

I nod.

Vance smiles.

"And now you think I'm an idiot. I mean, I am one, but now you know it too."

His thumb rubs over my cheek. "Oh, Quinnie, honey, my clueless boy ... I already knew you were an idiot."

I burst out laughing. "I really am. And I'm sorry. Again."

"I appreciate the apology, and not going to lie, I'm happy that snippy Quinn isn't the real you, but I need to ask ..."

I'm terrified of what's about to come out of his mouth.

"Why do you think anyone else's relationship in any way would reflect ours? Every relationship is different."

"I know. But ... just ... and, uh, with the ..." I sigh. "It's another stupid thing that I shouldn't say."

"Please say it?"

"Everything is so easy between us, like it's too good to be true, and you're perfect, and I'm ... me."

"This isn't some insecure you're not good enough to be with me kind of deal, is it? Because I have to say, neither of us are perfect, but I'm really beginning to believe we might be perfect for each other."

And I think I just fell in love with him.

When I don't have a response—not a coherent one anyway—he kisses me softly, and I fall even deeper.

He pulls back way too soon for me though. "Now, get your ass out of bed, and get to the arena for your morning skate before our flight to Seattle. You have a Stanley Cup to win tomorrow night."

Now that we've had this out though, I'm fucking terrified I've just ruined our chances.

"Don't give me that look. Nothing has changed. You didn't send out a curse to the hockey gods just because you managed to have a grown-up conversation with your boyfriend. Stop being a drama queen, take a deep breath, and win."

"You're right. Superstition shmuperstition."

—

Didn't curse the hockey gods, my ass.

There is no coming back from this clusterfuck of a bloodbath. There's a high chance we're going out with a shutout, and even though I tell myself we still have the next two games, the bigger part of my brain is telling me I fucked the team. This is all my fault because I stopped being irrationally snippy at my boyfriend.

And yes, I know how fucking absurd that sounds.

We're a disaster out there, not just crumbling under the pressure but fucking imploding from it.

We've barely made any shots on goal, and the ones we have made were easy saves.

They're killing us.

I don't think we've had a shutout all playoffs. To have it on the first chance at taking the Cup fills me with all kinds of doubt. And I'm sure I'm not the only one.

When the final buzzer for this shitshow goes off, we all trudge to the locker rooms, our heads held low because that was an embarrassment. No, worse than an embarrassment. That was … there are no words for it.

"Okay," Coach says calmly as he addresses us all. "So, we screwed the pooch on that one, but it's done now. Put it behind us and move on because we still have a chance here. More than a chance."

Putting it behind us is easier said than done.

This is the advantage Seattle needs to even the score and take this series to a game seven. After that, I'm sure all the bookies and betting sites are going crazy, fixing the odds to be in Seattle's favor.

Asher punches my arm. "Shake it off. We'll get it back."

I fucking hope so.

I replay the entire game over in my head on a loop, trying to pinpoint where we went wrong. Because something definitely went fucking wrong.

I'm still thinking about it when we get home to Buffalo.

Words are barely spoken the whole day between the team and between Vance and me. I know he wants to try to cheer me up, but nothing is going to get through to me.

Which is why, after a restless night's sleep, I'm woken by Vance throwing my suit pants at me, I'm confused. The anger in his face is unexpected.

"You're leaving your crap all over the place."

I frown. "Huh?" I am not awake enough for this.

"Your house is a mess. You're a mess. You … umm …" He glances around the room. "Your walls are an ugly beige color."

I look at the paint job. Yeah, he's right about that. "What are we doing here?"

"I'm trying to pick a fight so you can go back to being distracted on the ice for your next game."

It takes a second for it to sink in, but then it does, and holy shit, I let out the loudest snort I probably ever have. "I fucking love you so much."

Vance freezes. "You who in the what now?"

"Ah … sorry. Is that too soon?"

"No, it's … wow. Here I am trying to fight with you, and you've completely done a one-eighty."

"I just keep thinking about how you handled my diva behavior and that you're so patient with me, and even now, picking silly fights because, in my brain, us fighting made me play so well."

His whole expression softens. "What can I say? I think I must love you too. There's no one else I'd pick a fake fight with to make them feel better."

I pout to hide my smile because he just said he loves me too. "I can't believe you called me messy though. You're going to pay for that."

"Yeah? How?"

I throw the blanket off me, revealing my very naked body. "Pretend angry sex."

Vance jumps on top of me. "I hate you. I hate you so much."

"I hate you too. Let me show your ass just how much."

CHAPTER THIRTY

VANCE

Quinn doesn't give himself enough credit for just how amazing he is. Clueless and naïve are two words that get thrown around a lot, but I don't know many men who are confident enough in themselves to throw out the "L" word just because they feel it. It's one of the reasons he was so awkward initially; Quinn lets himself feel things, and he doesn't try to hold back.

His facial hair scrapes my thighs as he drops open-mouthed kisses along the sensitive skin, distracting me as he preps my hole. I love lying back and letting him take over, love seeing Quinn take some rare control as I card my fingers through his hair.

"You're a terrible, terrible person." I moan. "The way you … umm …"

He sniggers before he catches himself. "You can talk. You're a … a buttface."

"You're a *total* buttface."

"The buttest face that ever faced."

He engulfs my cock, and I shudder. "You didn't even fold your clothes. Why are you so messy?"

"Should I stop and do it now?" he asks, pulling off with a grin.

"No. I'm just mad at you. So ... *so* mad."

Quinn brushes his fingers over my prostate, and my toes curl. "How mad?"

"I hate you so much."

He laughs into my hip crease, and I tug his hair until he's looking at me again. "How is it possible that we can't even fake fight?"

"No, no. I'm sorry. You're doing good. Keep going."

"Yesterday, you said you liked or-eh-geno in your pasta sauce. Instead of oregano. You called it or-eh-geno." It was adorable hearing it so mispronounced.

"And now you're making fun of how I talk?" he gasps, fingers disappearing from my ass and leaving me empty.

"Sorr—"

Quinn's hand slaps down over my mouth. "How fucking dare you?"

Mmph. The heat in his eyes, the slight rasp to his voice. He moves his hand, and I growl out, "I've seen the memes people post about you online. Disgusting."

"What about you? Bet you've felt up every one of my teammates, haven't you?"

"I get paid to do it too."

Quinn shoves me onto my front, and I go willingly. Then his lean body is covering my back, sheathed cock dragging over my ass cheek. "I'm going to fuck you so hard you forget every one of them."

"I'd like to see you try." I'd really, *really* like it.

He grunts, reaching down to position himself before pressing forward. The second he breaches me, he snaps his hips forward, sealing us together with one thrust.

"My hole," he rumbles.

"Only if you learn how to rinse your fucking dishes."

"At least I can close the lid on the sauce bottles."

"You just forget how to hang your towels in the bathroom."

Quinn flexes his hips, pushing himself as deep as he can go. It's a beautiful goddamn burn, being stuffed full of him, stretched around his cock so tight I feel every movement. Quinn holds me pinned to the bed, mouth right by my ear.

"Even though you didn't vacuum today, I still love the way you feel wrapped around me."

"Mmm, talk dirty to me."

He chuckles, starting to roll his hips, teasing me with the delicious slide of his cock in and out of me. Quinn's hitting all the right places, making me feel tingly and delicious. And sure, we might suck at the fighting thing, but I've officially gotten him out of his head and forgetting about the game, which was my only aim for tonight.

I'll let him fuck me any day if it helps him forget about hockey.

"I hate that you're so perfect," he pants, hot breaths hitting my hairline. "That you don't make it easy on me or my poor heart."

"Good. If you love me as much as I love you, I'm torturing you the exact right amount."

"Do I torture you?"

"Constantly. You're an asshole for it. Being so fun and so sweet and so scorching hot. Not letting me touch you in public for so long."

"But you can now."

"That's the one thing I'm not mad at you about."

He groans, driving in faster. Quinn's large hands seek out where mine are gripping the sheets, and his fingers slide through mine. I melt against the bed, his body, the way he's leaving soft, slow kisses along my shoulder.

"You know, I could be wrong, but I feel like hate-sexing needs a whole lot more hate and a whole lot less love."

He smiles against my skin. "Should I ask Ez for tips?"

I cringe. "Don't mention your friends while your cock's inside me."

"Why? Most people would love to think of Ezra Palaszczuk while they're getting off."

"Do *you*?"

"Would it bother you if I did?"

I grunt, shoving back against him. "Yes, it fucking would."

"Well, you don't need to worry about that because even if Anton Hayes didn't terrify me, ever since I met you, I haven't been able to think of anyone else. Why do you think I went dry for so long? Thanks for that, asshole."

"Oooh, you sound mad."

"I am mad."

"Then prove it."

Then Quinn completely surprises me by biting down into my shoulder. His hips snap forward, setting a punishing pace, and thank the fucking fucks for this man's stamina because he doesn't let up. His hands squeeze around mine, hips slapping against my ass, the telltale rhythmic bang of the bed hitting the wall.

My cock is swollen and aching, sliding against the sheets, begging me to take hold of it, but I can't. With my hands pinned and Quinn controlling the angle, I'm not coming until he wants me to.

The heat where our skin meets is blazing, sweat prickling all over me, Quinn's grunts hot and heavy in my ear, sending desperate want slithering into my gut.

"Come on," I whine, out of my fucking mind. "I need … I need to come …"

"You'll wait until I'm goddamn finished," he hisses, and it almost sets me off.

Pressure is building in my groin, making everything oversensitive, and Quinn pegging my prostate over and over has made me lose all feeling in my legs.

He cries out, shoving upward suddenly, hands landing on my shoulders as his hips go still, and his cock throbs out his release into the condom. He doesn't take a second to catch his breath, just pulls out, rolls us onto our sides, then fills my ass with his fingers and jerks me off with the other. I want to sob at how good it feels, how much I needed the friction, and even though I give it my best shot to hold off, my dick has other ideas.

A few strokes and it's all over. My cock swells in his hand, and I unload all over his fist and my abs.

Then I sink back against him as I catch my breath.

He holds me close, nose buried in my hair, and when I come down enough to find reality again, I scoff.

"Well, now you've done it. Look at this mess you've made." I shake my head. "You're the worst."

"No, you're the worst."

I smile, eyes falling closed. "I still love you, asshole."

"You too, dickhead."

—

I keep up our stupid, petty fight as much as possible the morning before Quinn has to leave. I purposely leave the milk on the counter, throw his blankets on the floor in the bedroom, and leave my half-eaten breakfast on the coffee table. Quinn huffs and puffs like the big bad wolf and looks adorable while doing it. By the time he leaves for his warm-up skate, I think he's happy to be rid of me. Not that he probably needed the extra incentive. If they win tonight, that's it. Season over.

And after how he played last game, I'll bet he's overly conscious of that fact.

I am too.

The last thing I want after him turning the season around is to see him choke last minute. Even if they don't—I can't even think the word—I still want him to be able to walk away knowing he played the best game he could.

Another shutout? No fucking way. Not happening.

Shit. I'm so sick I can't even finish my coffee, so I have no idea how the players are handling this.

We haven't been to playoffs in *ten years*, have never made it to a final, and here we are, on the brink of the Stanley fucking Cup. I don't think anyone in the Buffalo camp knows how to handle this moment, but it's hitting me a thousand percent harder knowing that the man I love has everything riding on this.

Cup or not, I don't care. But I know it'd kill him to come this close and walk away empty-handed. It'd kill any of them, frankly, but I'm finding it hard to spare sympathy for Aleks or Bilson. I can give them my commiserations later.

I pace the house, cleaning up because while I want to get in his head and stay there for the game, I'm too fucking nervous not to be doing anything. After the guys have their morning skate, they'll be leaving for the airport to head to Seattle, and all three of us trainers will be going with them. I wish we were leaving now because I feel fucking useless.

I need this game to get started already.

CHAPTER THIRTY-ONE

QUINN

"Throwing up on the ice would be bad for my image, wouldn't it?" I ask Asher as we stand for the national anthem. I know he's nervous when he doesn't even have a smartass remark.

The starting lineup is out on the ice while the rest of us are in the team box, hands on hearts, and I refuse to look at any of the Seattle players. My gaze is firmly on the US flag hanging from the rafters.

We can't choke again. They have the chance to even it up to three games apiece tonight if we don't take them down.

Then it'll all come down to the final game.

Nope, nope, nope, can't let that happen.

As the puck drops, so does my stomach. I will not vomit. I will not vomit.

We all watch the ice intently, holding our breaths when Seattle takes a shot on goal and getting out of our seats when our teammates do.

It's a fight from the beginning, both teams dragging out the first goal, both goalies using their lightning-fast reflexes to save the bullets being shot at them.

I'm so distracted with watching the ice I don't hear the tapping on the glass behind me. Asher has to nudge me and point it out.

I turn, and there's Vance, concerned look on his face.

"Focus on me," he says. "When you're out there. Don't think. Just do. Oh, and ..." He takes his hand out of his pocket and flips me the bird.

It both relaxes me and puts me in the right mindset to get out there.

Even if I'm silently shitting myself about being the first line to let a goal past us.

When we're tapped to get out there, it's not the best shift in the world, but we manage to keep Seattle from scoring, so I'm taking it as a win.

Play is slow. And by slow, I mean superfast. It's slow because neither team is getting the edge. Seattle is desperate to hold on to hope, and we're desperate to end this.

The first period ends with no one managing to put one in the net, and I get the distinct feeling this is going to be a long, long night.

In the second, Samry manages to put one away for us, which eases my guts but not enough. I'm not being greedy when wanting a bigger lead. I just want to put as much distance between us and them.

We have numerous shifts where nothing happens. We get close, they get close, but it's almost like we're playing a game of chicken, seeing who's going to crack first.

The clock is winding down on the second period when Coach sends us back out there, and as I get the puck and pass to Asher, I think I've miscalculated. I can see it happening in slow motion. Katz from Seattle is right on top of it. He's going to intercept.

My gut sinks, and I get checked from behind by a mammoth of a defenseman. I hit the ice, but I don't take my eye off that puck.

I have no fucking idea where Asher gets enough speed, but he ekes out Katz, shoots, and puts the puck in the fucking net.

And the best part? We get a fucking power play, thanks to me being pummeled, and Müller follows up an Asher goal with one of his own.

This. This is the fucking team we needed to be.

Now all we have to do is fucking hold on to the 3-0 lead for one more damn period.

During our break in between periods, Vance, Boone, and O'Hennessy tape, massage, and ice our boo-boos while Coach gives us a "This is your moment" speech.

I really fucking hope it's our moment, but the pressure is piling on, even with the lead we have.

I can see it all falling and crumbling because it's what Buffalo does. We're known for it. We showed it in the last game.

I'm getting in my head again, and Vance must be able to tell because he drops down in front of me and puts his hand on my thigh.

"How are you doing? You okay? How's the adductor?"

"It's fine." I've had minor twinges here and there since the playoffs started, but we've been monitoring it, and it's all good so far. I might have lifelong pain from the tear and the way it healed, but we're professional athletes. Aches and pains are normal for what we put our bodies through.

"How's your head?"

"Haven't had any complaints. You tell me." I grin.

"Okay, that's good. You haven't lost your ability to joke."

"No, but I am in it a little bit."

"I noticed. To which I only have one thing to say to you. No, two. You do realize you let your linemates show you up, right? They get a goal, and you're sitting on two measly assists? Pull your head out of your ass."

"That seemed like a lot more than two things, but I appreciate you being mean to me."

Vance leans in close. "The other thing was I love you, and you've got this."

I want to close the small gap between us and touch my lips to his, but it's not exactly the most professional space to do it in—for either of us.

Walking back out to the team box is daunting, and as I glance up at the big screens showing ours and Seattle's faces, I have to say we look scared shitless while Seattle looks fired up.

Three goals in one period is no easy feat, but it's definitely doable.

And right out the gate, Aleks gets possession of the puck and scores less than a minute into the fucking period.

"Can we kick Aleksander Emerson out of the Collective?" I ask Asher.

"It's only one."

It's not only one.

Cody Bilson puts another away five minutes later.

It's happening.

We're fucking choking.

Neither team manages to score again, and while we're still one up, we're only one Seattle goal away from going into overtime.

Vance's words play back through my head, and surprisingly, it isn't the taunting me about not getting a goal that I remember. His faith in me, his love—the way he said, "I love you, and you've got this"—is.

We're sent over the side for our shift, and with all the love in my heart and the Vance distraction in my head, I play for him.

And I get that fucking goal.

4–2 with less than a minute on the clock?

Buffalo has just won their first-ever Stanley Cup.

—

Ezra holds up his glass as he toasts, "To the Cup going to the Collective again!"

Asher, beside me, mutters, "Yes, because the entire Collective is responsible for those goals."

The after-party with the team happened right after the game, but now we're having the official Queer Collective celebration at my place.

"And to Asher," Westly Dalton, Asher's older brother and the one he gets compared to all the time, says. "For going out his rookie year and taking the championship."

Asher cocks his head. "What, like it's hard?"

There's a round of boos from everyone in the room, but it only makes Asher laugh.

Foster steps forward. "Can we all please just enjoy this moment where we relive learning, for maybe the first time, that Asher Dalton has a heart?" He hits Play on his phone, and it's the clip of Asher at the press conference after we won.

Someone had the balls to ask him about his brother West, but instead of his scowl before cussing them out, he lets out a genuine smile and says, "All I know is I wouldn't be where I am today if it weren't for him, and I'm grateful that he's an amazing and supportive big brother."

Now it's Asher's turn to boo.

"You love me," West sings. "You really looooove me."

"People kill those they love all the time. Don't think you're immune to it."

A round of "Aww"s fills the room because no one's going to believe Asher anymore when he threatens violence.

I wrap my arm around his shoulders. "You're just a lovebug underneath."

"Permission to change Little D's nickname to Love Bug?" Ezra asks.

"Fuck no," Asher growls.

"Approved!" West says at the same time.

We might be a group of completely egotistical, irresponsible, shameless, foolish, and clueless fuckboys, but I wouldn't change any of them for the world.

We raise our glasses and cheers to the motherfucking Stanley Cup.

EPILOGUE

VANCE

"I'm telling you," Anton starts, "you don't want to give Ezra the idea of a queer puppy rescue hockey team. Just, don't. Even *I'm* tempted, but just because Dog Tripp has been all over the dudes doesn't mean the gay agenda is that strong. And honestly, I'd like to spend some time with my boyfriend this off-season." He goes to take a drink before adding, "*Not* rescuing dogs."

"Save the hero work for Gabe," Aleks adds.

Quinn comes inside the enormous cabin the Queer Collective have rented for the week. It turns out the sneaky butthead had bought my plane ticket for this thing all along. The place is surrounded by trees, and I can make out the sound of the waves at the beach down the end of the short trail.

Not everyone could make it, but Tripp and Dex came for two days before heading home since Tripp's sister is about to give birth to their second nibling. Oskar and Lane will be arriving sometime tomorrow, just in time for the weekend. Asher's home with his family, and one of the retired members is supposed to be showing up later today.

The rest of the week, it's been Aleks and Gabe, Ezra and Anton, and Foster and Zach. But the only guy I've cared about is the one giving me a wide smile as he joins me on the couch.

Or, at least, I think I've only got eyes for him when there's a commotion from around the side, and Ezra shouts, "Soren!"

A minute later, Ezra and Caleb Sorenson come into view—along with Soren's husband.

"Jay ... Jay ... Jay Jackson?" I'm aware of how stupid I sound, but holy fucking shit. One of my favorite rock stars is standing feet away.

A smirk crosses his handsome face. "Hey. It's about time one of Soren's friends gave me the greeting I deserve."

Ezra snorts. "I *offered* you an orgy. What, like that's not enough for you?"

"And I *offered* you a black eye," Soren throws back. "That's still on the table, anytime you want it."

Anton grabs Ezra's waist and pulls him into his lap, and whatever he says into Ezra's ear has the man melting. Dear fucking God, the evil that must exist in one person to be able to control Ezra fucking Palaszczuk.

My wide eyes swing back to Jay Jackson, unable to believe he's here.

Zach sighs. "I think he wants an autograph but is being too polite to ask."

"I promise I'm not normally this uncool," I squeak. But I can't be sure of that at all because when Jay Jackson flops down on the couch on the other side of me and slings his arm around my shoulder, I'm a giddy mess.

"Photos are better," Jay Jackson says. "My face is prettier than my scribble."

I'm scrambling for my phone before I can ask if he's sure.

"Someone's not happy," Ezra sings.

I take a photo and turn to where Quinn has his arms crossed, pout on his gorgeous face. "I thought I liked you, but I've changed my mind," he says to Jay Jackson.

"I have that effect on people."

And seeing Quinn all jealous over my fanboying just makes this day a thousand times better. Having a man who never tries to hide how he feels about me is an incredible high I'll never be used to.

"Aww, baby." I try to pull Quinn into my lap, but he stands and pulls me up with him instead.

"I was making something for you earlier, but now I don't know if I want to give it to you."

"Ooh, you wanna fight instead?"

He laughs. "Not in off-season. No fighting allowed."

"Then you have no choice but to show me."

"Fiiine." Quinn drags me outside, pretending to be exasperated, but I can tell he's excited by whatever it is. The voices behind us fade, and even knowing that one of my favorite singers is only a few feet away doesn't make me want to do anything but follow Quinn. He's a thousand Jay Jacksons any day.

"Where are you …" My words trail off when we walk a couple of feet into the woods, where a thin stream runs.

Quinn's found some wooden logs and balanced them across the stream, then tied them together with rope. It's barely long enough for us to both stand on it side by side, and while I'm worried about the thing collapsing under our weight, when he pulls me out after him, it doesn't shift.

"You made me a bridge."

He fucking beams at me. "It's nothing like the Queensboro Bridge—"

"It's perfect."

He huffs a laugh. "I still maintain you are. It's just … sometimes I don't feel like I give you enough when you're always so amazing to me. You pick fights if I need to fight. You're constantly checking on my leg. You came on this trip just because I said I wanted you here—"

"And you'd already bought the ticket—"

"That too. But even if I hadn't, we both know you wouldn't have said no. Sometimes it feels like you go out of your way to make everything so easy."

"Relationships don't *have* to be hard though."

"No, I know." He wraps his arms around me. "I just want you to know that while I might not be as thoughtful and constant as you at giving you what you need, I'll always try. I know the bridge isn't a lot, but it's more the symbol of it. It's where we started. It's something you like. Whenever I see a bridge, whether it's huge and impressive or a thrown-together mess, I'll think of you. And hopefully, we'll have all the time in the world for me to take you to all the bridges in the world. This one is just the first."

He thinks this isn't a lot? The fact he thought of something like this and did it just to show he was thinking of me is *everything*. "Grand gestures don't always have to be grand," I tell him. "You show me in other ways. The way you reach for me when you're sleeping. How you always ask my opinion on things. Watching shows with me that you don't really like, just because you know I like them. The way you are constantly trying things I love to do, to see what things we can do together. And this bridge. You missed time with your friends to put this together for me when you could have just done that whole speech without it. You don't only try, Quinn. You *do*. I see it, even if you don't."

He smiles and presses our lips together in a soft, slow kiss. "I know what my thing is," he whispers.

"What?"

"You. I know you said it shouldn't be another person, but I say fuck that. I want it to be you. I'm sure about you. We're it, Vancelicious, and whether that means my free time is looking up all the bridges we can visit together, or watching more shitty TV shows, or driving out to random geocaching locations, or picking fake fights, or begging another member of the Collective to bring his famous husband on the retreat because you're constantly playing his stupid songs, I'll do it. I have hockey, and I have you. And that's all I need to be happy."

I cup his face, wondering if it's possible to love him more than I already do. "Who said you were clueless at this relationship thing?"

"Literally everyone. But I'm a fast learner."

We head back to the house together, and I'm walking on goddamn clouds. More people have shown up; Asher and Kole, despite Asher's insistence that he'd rather die than spend more time with Ezra, and Asher's brother West. Apparently, his partner is looking after the Dalton siblings so West could get away for the weekend.

And seeing Quinn with them, seeing them all together, happy and out and wild, I'm hit with that same feeling I got when Asher and Quinn were playing Ezra and Anton. The sheer pride I feel to be a part of something like this is amazing, and maybe hockey and me aren't terrible things for Quinn to have.

But he's got these guys too.

And I have a feeling we'll both have them for the rest of our lives.